Mighty Mighty MONSTERS

Homesick Witch

STONE ARCH BOOKS
a capstone imprint

Mighty Mighty Monsters are published by
Stone Arch Books, A Capstone Imprint
1710 Roe Crest Drive
North Mankato, Minnesota 56003 www.
capstonepub.com

Library of Congress Cataloging-in-
Publication Data

ISBN: 978-1-4342-3893-1 (library binding)
ISBN: 978-1-4342-4225-9 (paperback)
ISBN: 978-1-4342-4648-6 (eBook)

Summary: Witchita is leaving for the
Salem School of Witchcraft, a special
school that will have her away for the
entire summer. The Mighty, Mighty
Monsters are sad to see her go, but
Witchita is excited to learn all new sorts
of witchery. A few days after she leaves,
they receive a letter from Wichita saying
that she's monstrously miserable! The
gang immediately hits the road to save
their sorrowful friend from summer
school.

Printed in the United States of America
in Stevens Point, Wisconsin.
032012
006678WZF12

3 7777 12234 4369

Mighty Mighty MONSTERS

Homesick Witch

created by
Sean O'Reilly

illustrated by
Arcana Studio

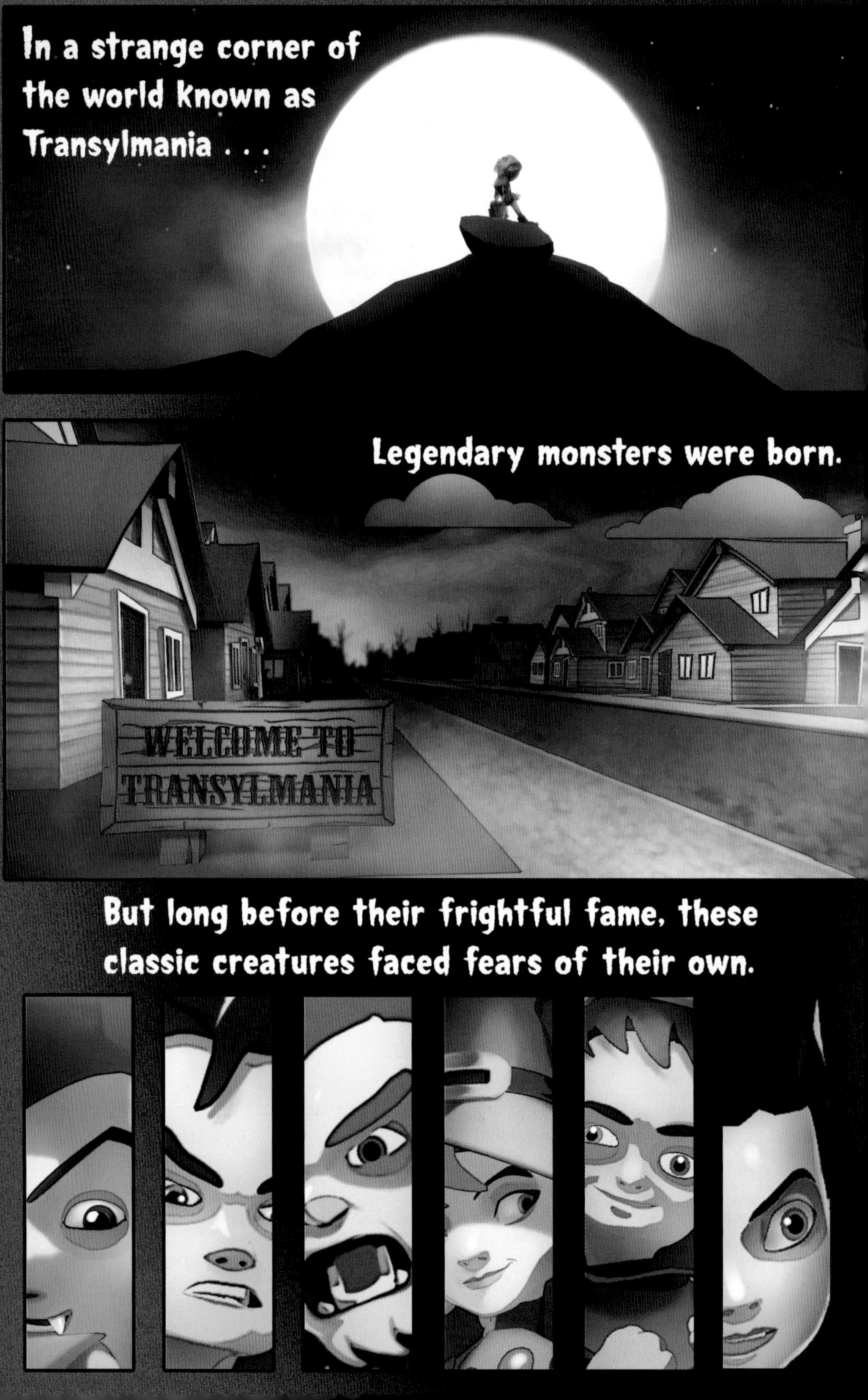
In a strange corner of the world known as Transylmania . . .
Legendary monsters were born.
WELCOME TO TRANSYLMANIA
But long before their frightful fame, these classic creatures faced fears of their own.

To take on terrifying teachers and homework horrors, they formed the most fearsome friendship on Earth . . .

Mighty Mighty MONSTERS

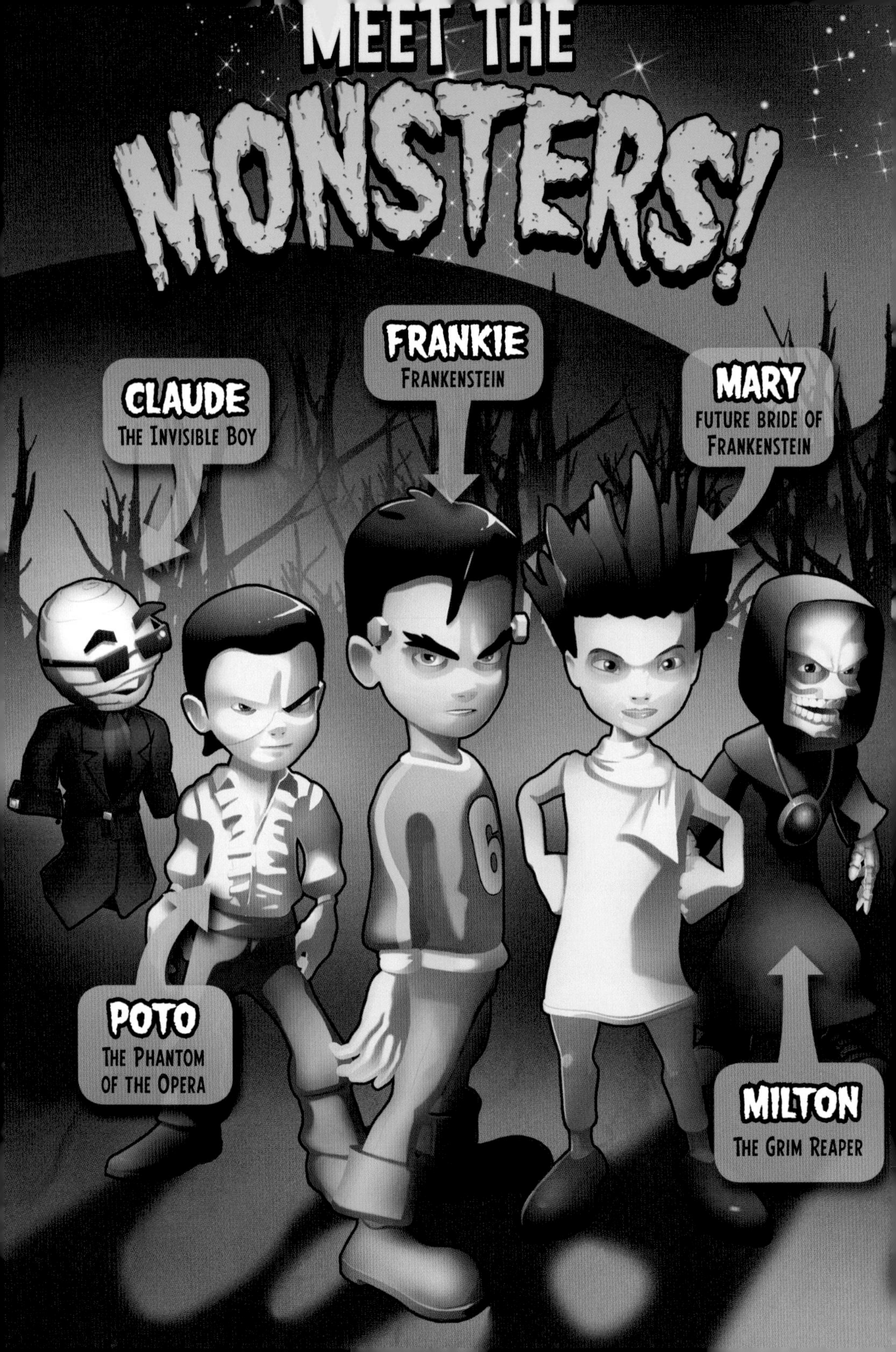
MEET THE MONSTERS!
FRANKIE
FRANKENSTEIN
CLAUDE
THE INVISIBLE BOY
MARY
FUTURE BRIDE OF FRANKENSTEIN
POTO
THE PHANTOM OF THE OPERA
MILTON
THE GRIM REAPER

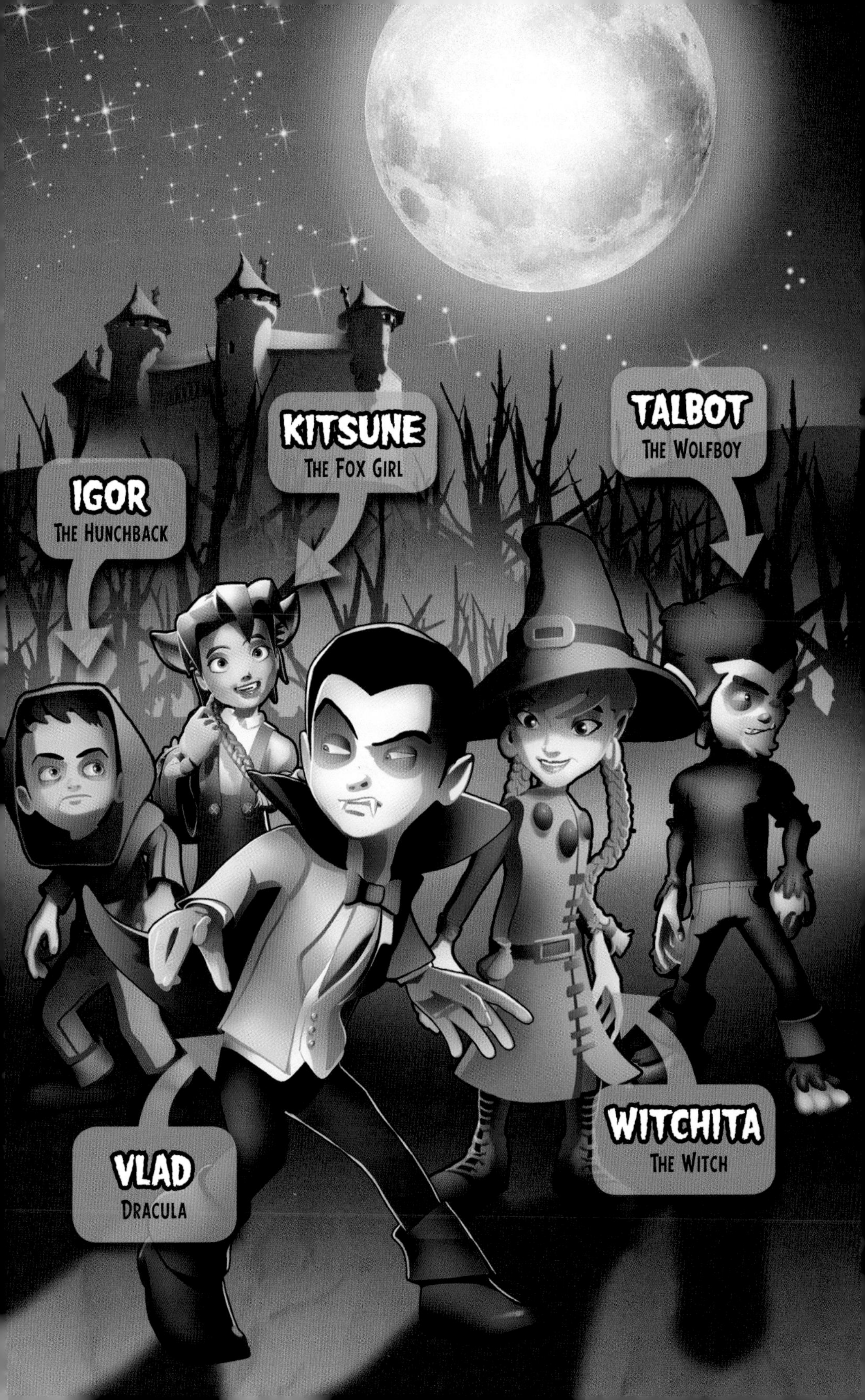
IGOR
THE HUNCHBACK
KITSUNE
THE FOX GIRL
TALBOT
THE WOLFBOY
VLAD
DRACULA
WITCHITA
THE WITCH

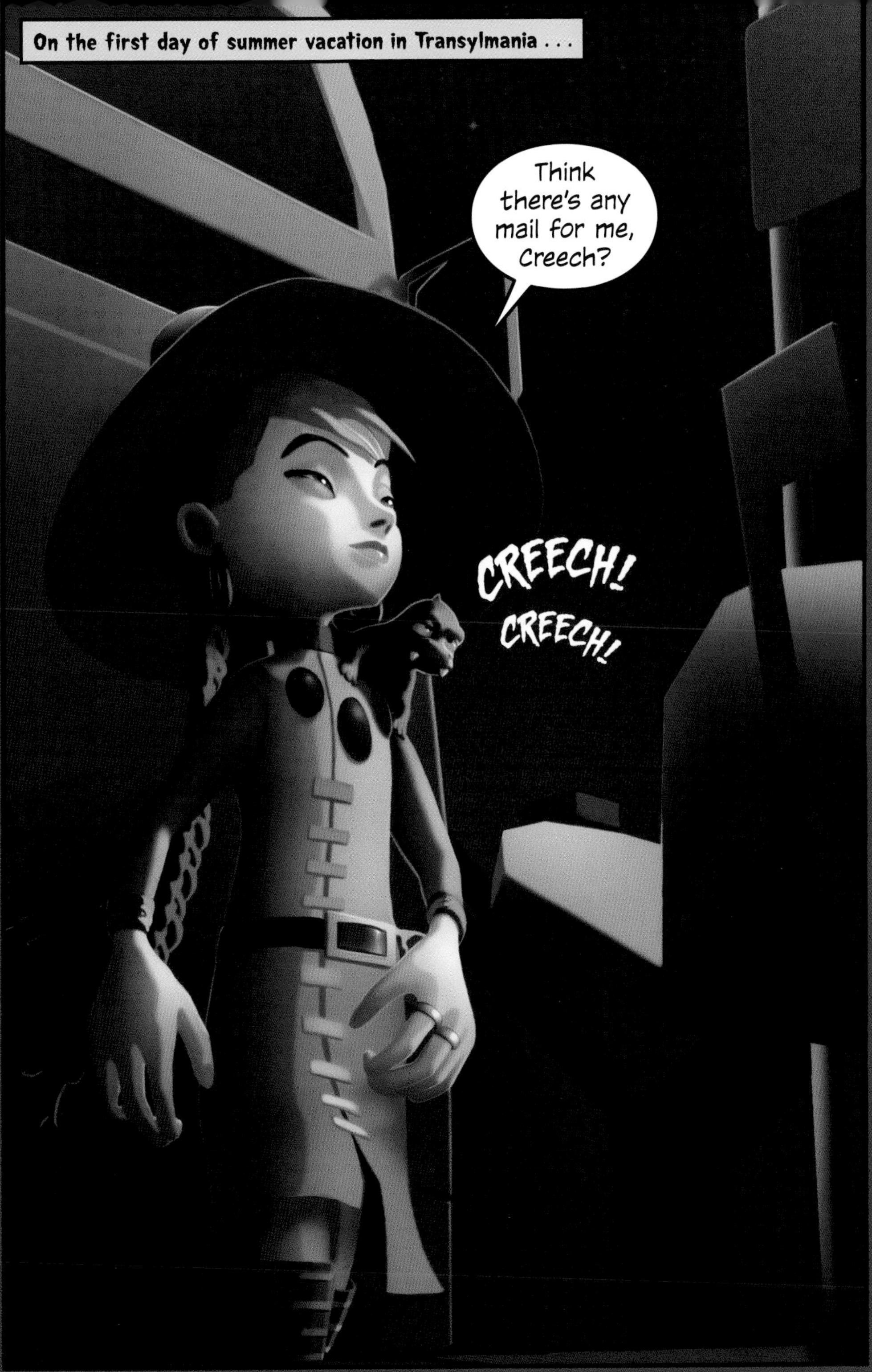
On the first day of summer vacation in Transylmania . . .
Think there's any mail for me, Creech?
CREECH!
CREECH!

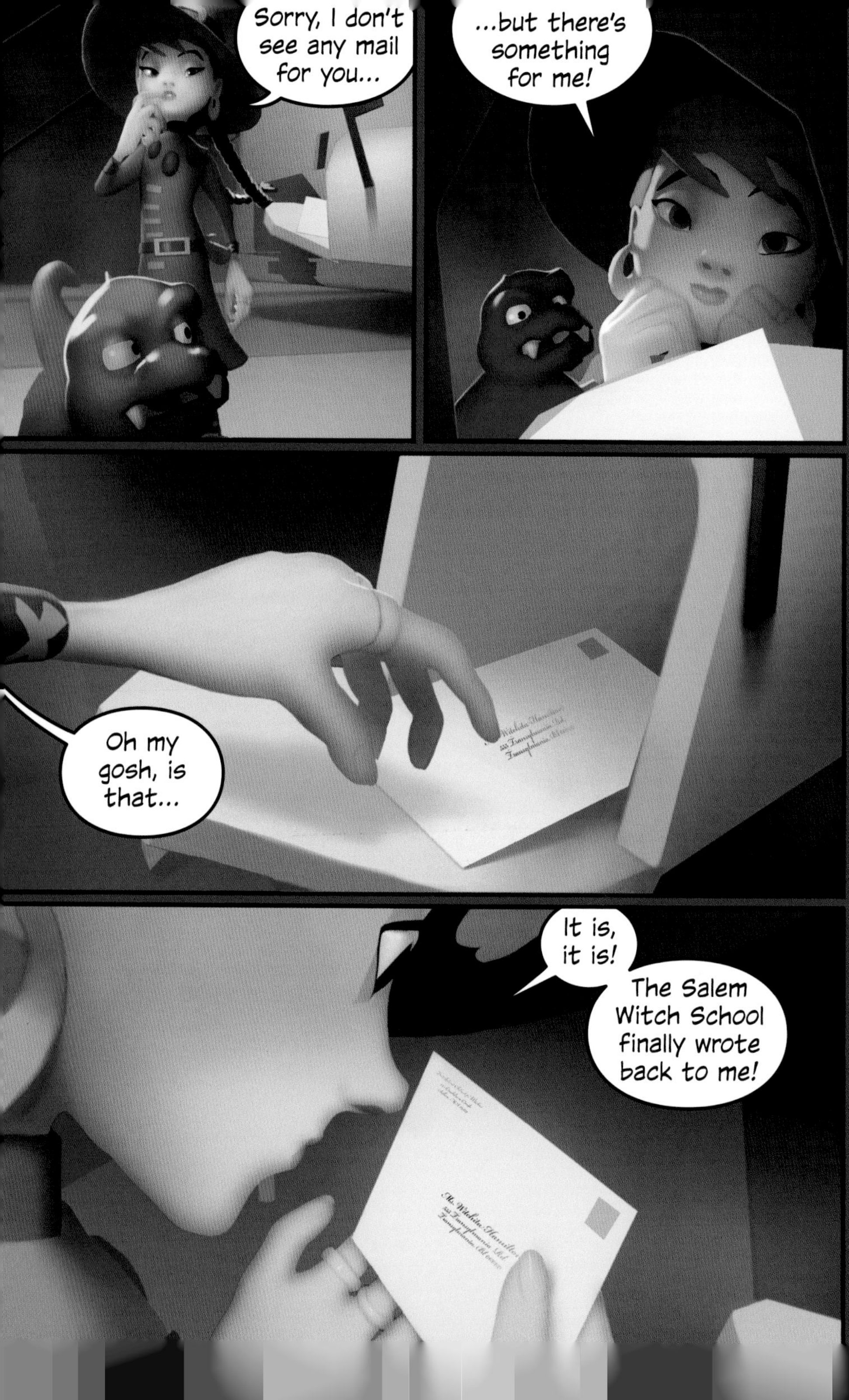
Sorry, I don't see any mail for you...
...but there's something for me!
Oh my gosh, is that...
It is, it is!
The Salem Witch School finally wrote back to me!

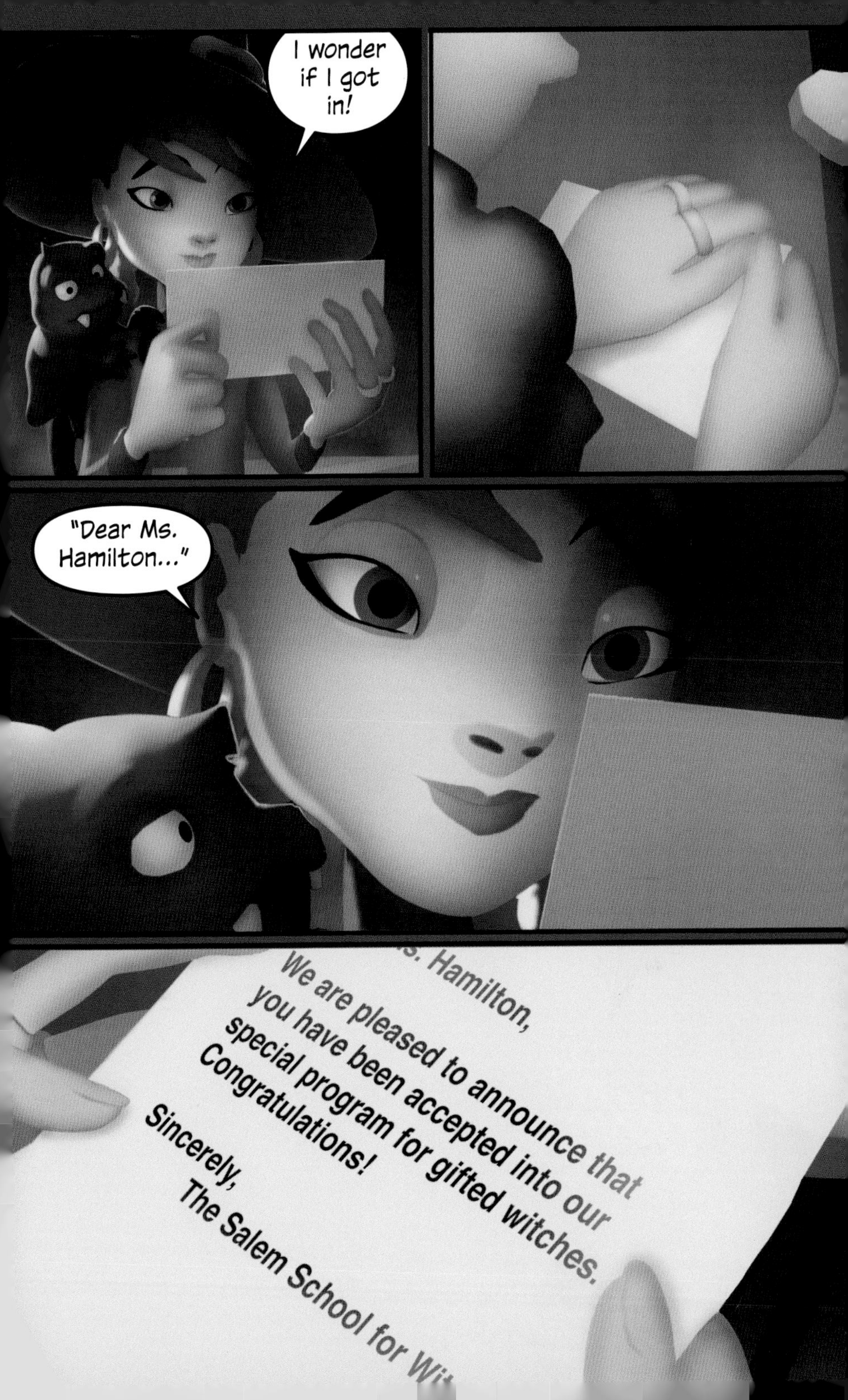
I wonder if I got in!
"Dear Ms. Hamilton..."
Hamilton,
We are pleased to announce that
you have been accepted into our
special program for gifted witches.
Congratulations!
Sincerely,
The Salem School for

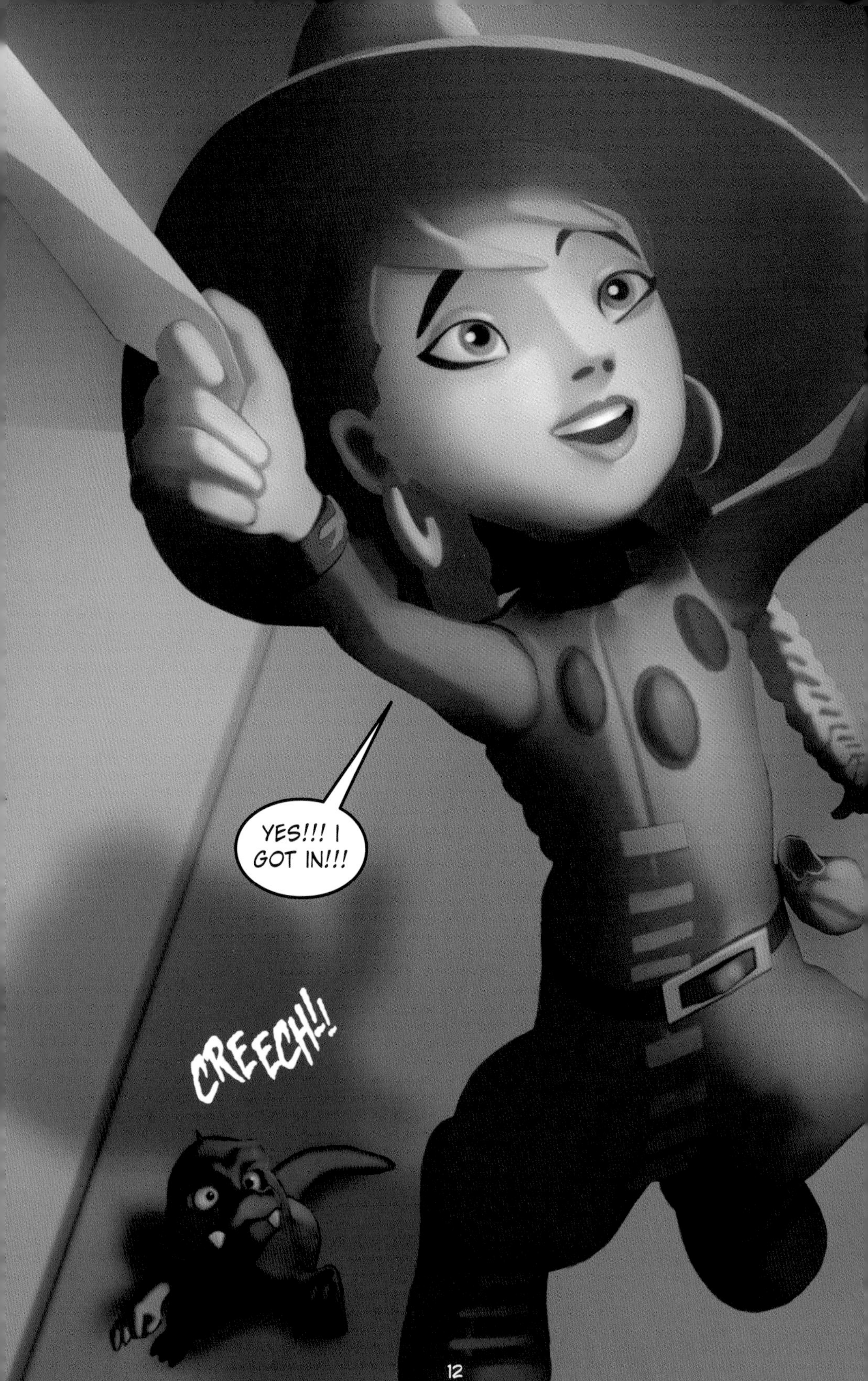
YES!!! I GOT IN!!!
CREECH!!!

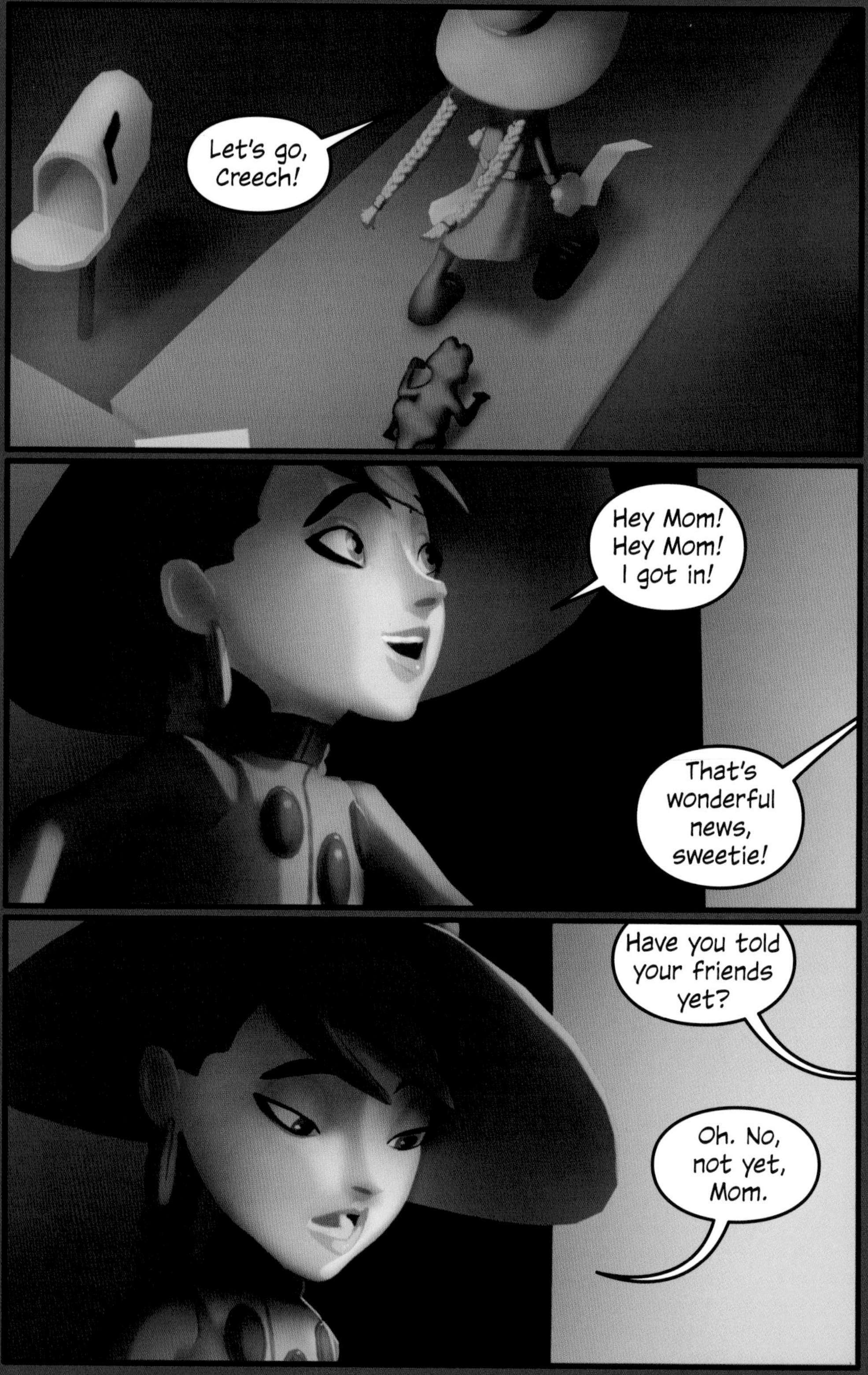
Let's go, Creech!
Hey Mom! Hey Mom! I got in!
That's wonderful news, sweetie!
Have you told your friends yet?
Oh. No, not yet, Mom.

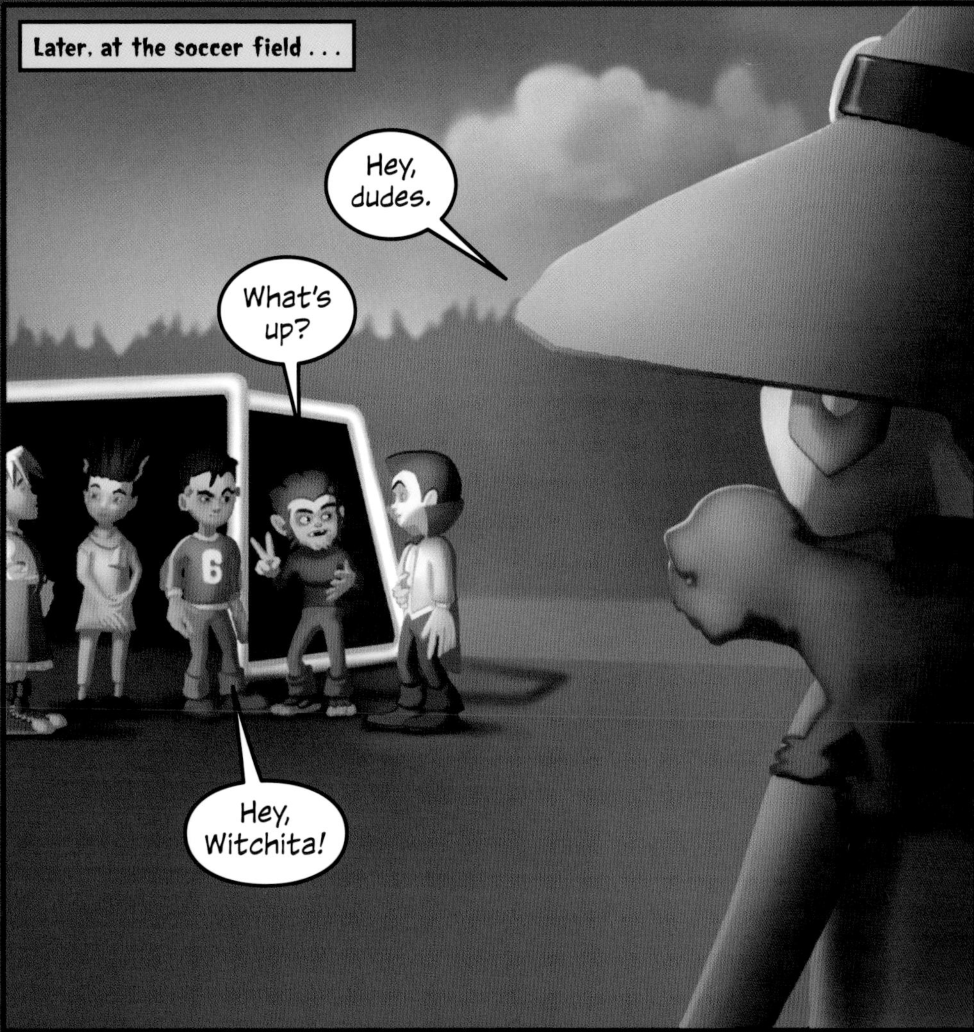
Later, at the soccer field . . .
Hey, dudes.
What's up?
Hey, Witchita!

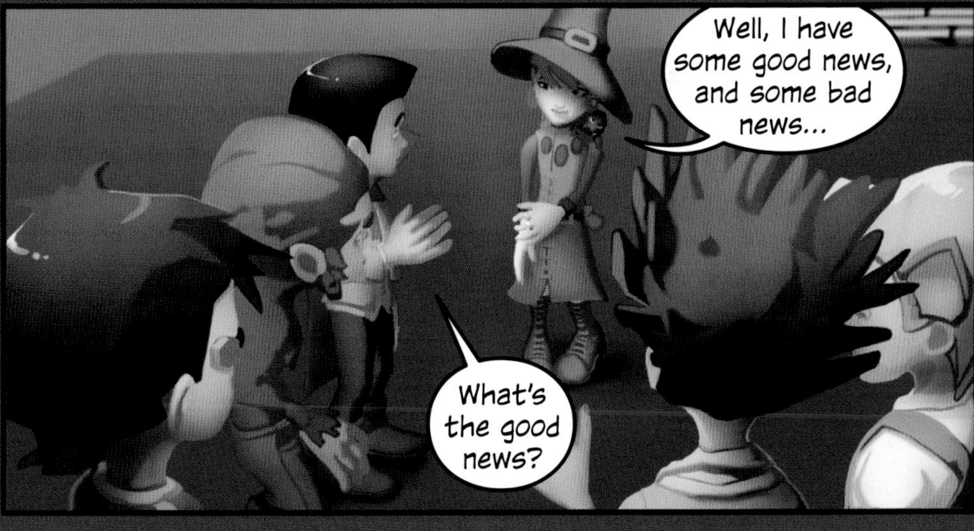
Well, I have some good news, and some bad news...
What's the good news?

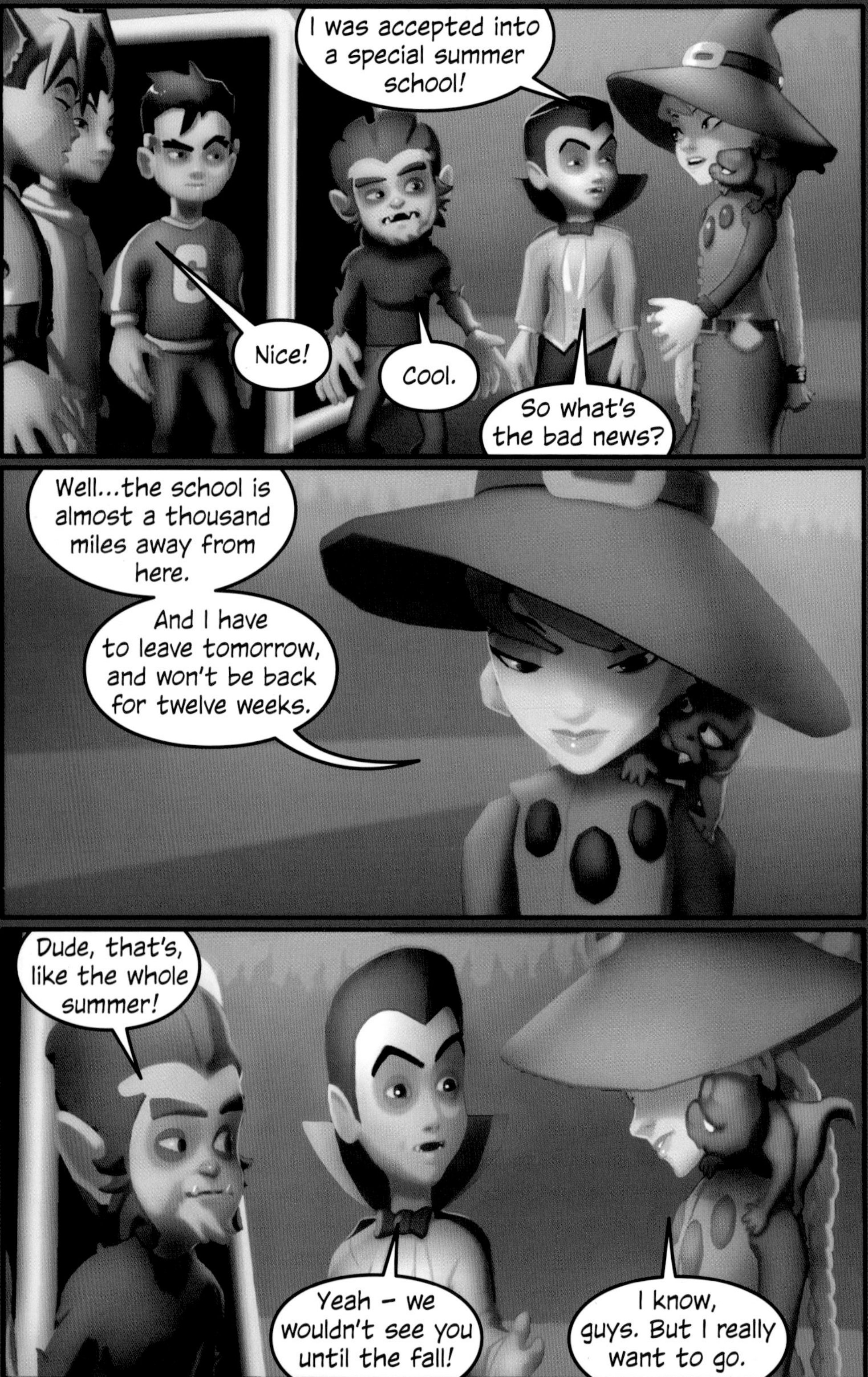

I was accepted into a special summer school!
Nice!
Cool.
So what's the bad news?
Well...the school is almost a thousand miles away from here.
And I have to leave tomorrow, and won't be back for twelve weeks.
Dude, that's, like the whole summer!
Yeah – we wouldn't see you until the fall!
I know, guys. But I really want to go.

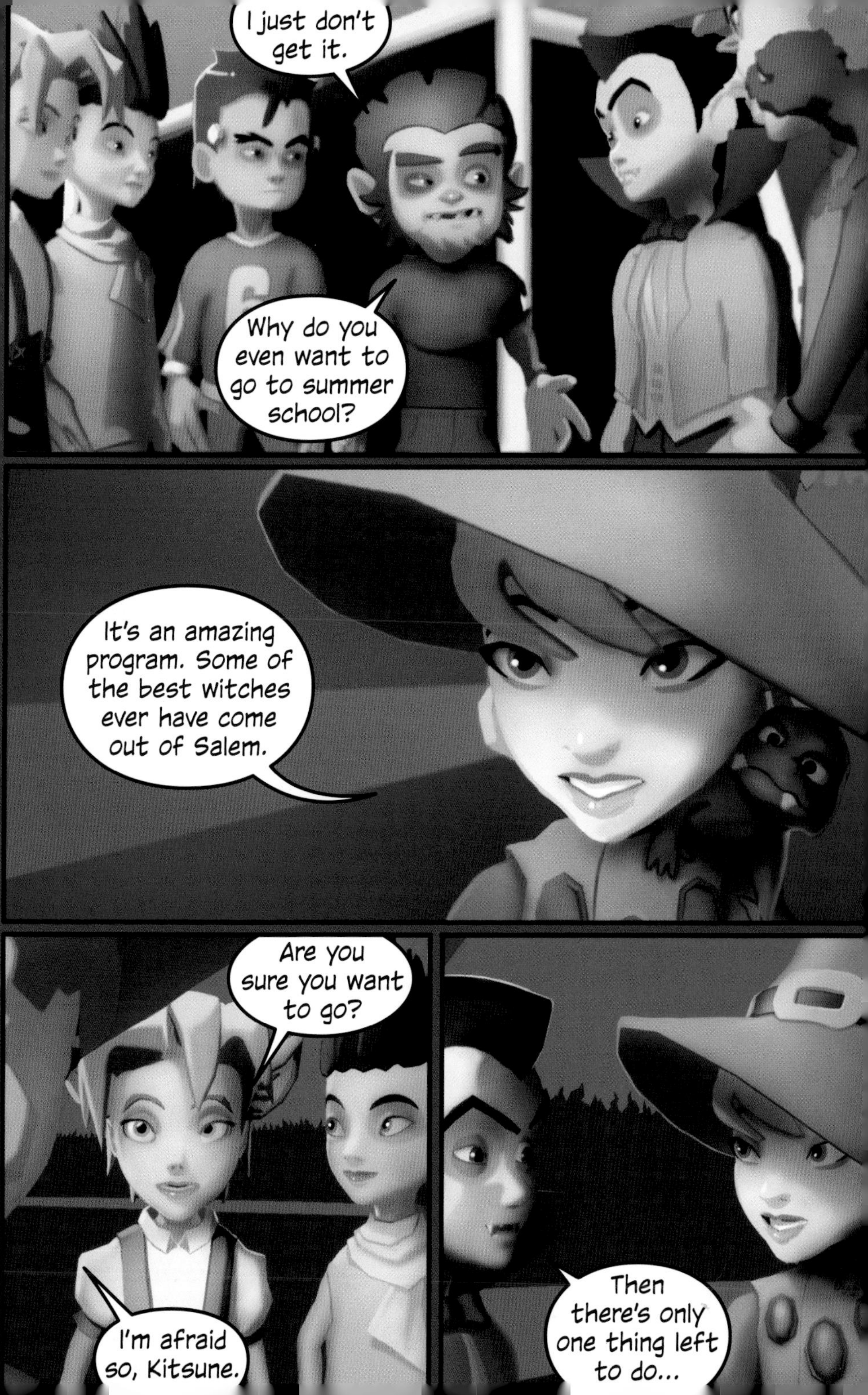
I just don't get it.
Why do you even want to go to summer school?
It's an amazing program. Some of the best witches ever have come out of Salem.
Are you sure you want to go?
I'm afraid so, Kitsune.
Then there's only one thing left to do...

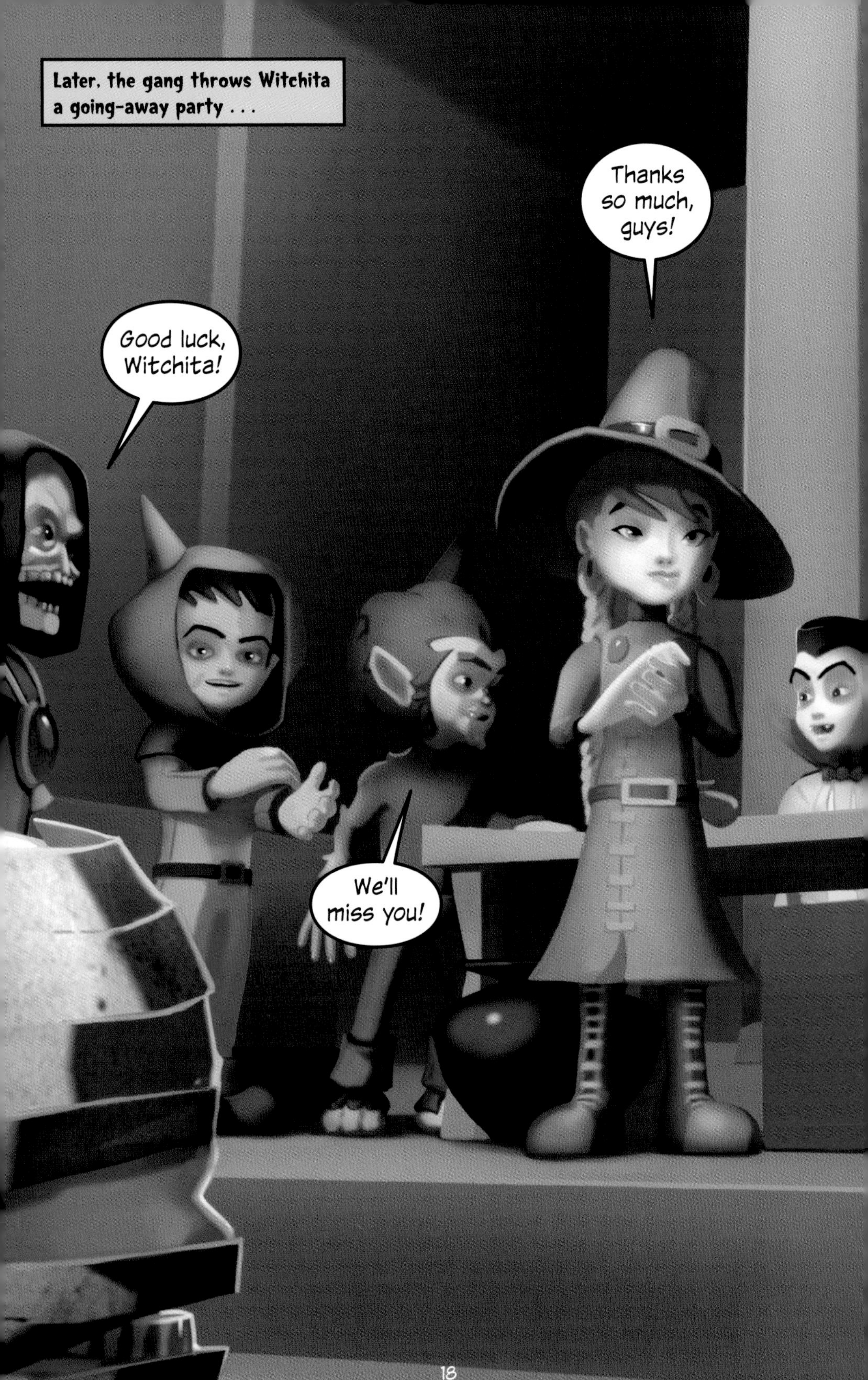
Later, the gang throws Witchita a going-away party . . .
Thanks so much, guys!
Good luck, Witchita!
We'll miss you!

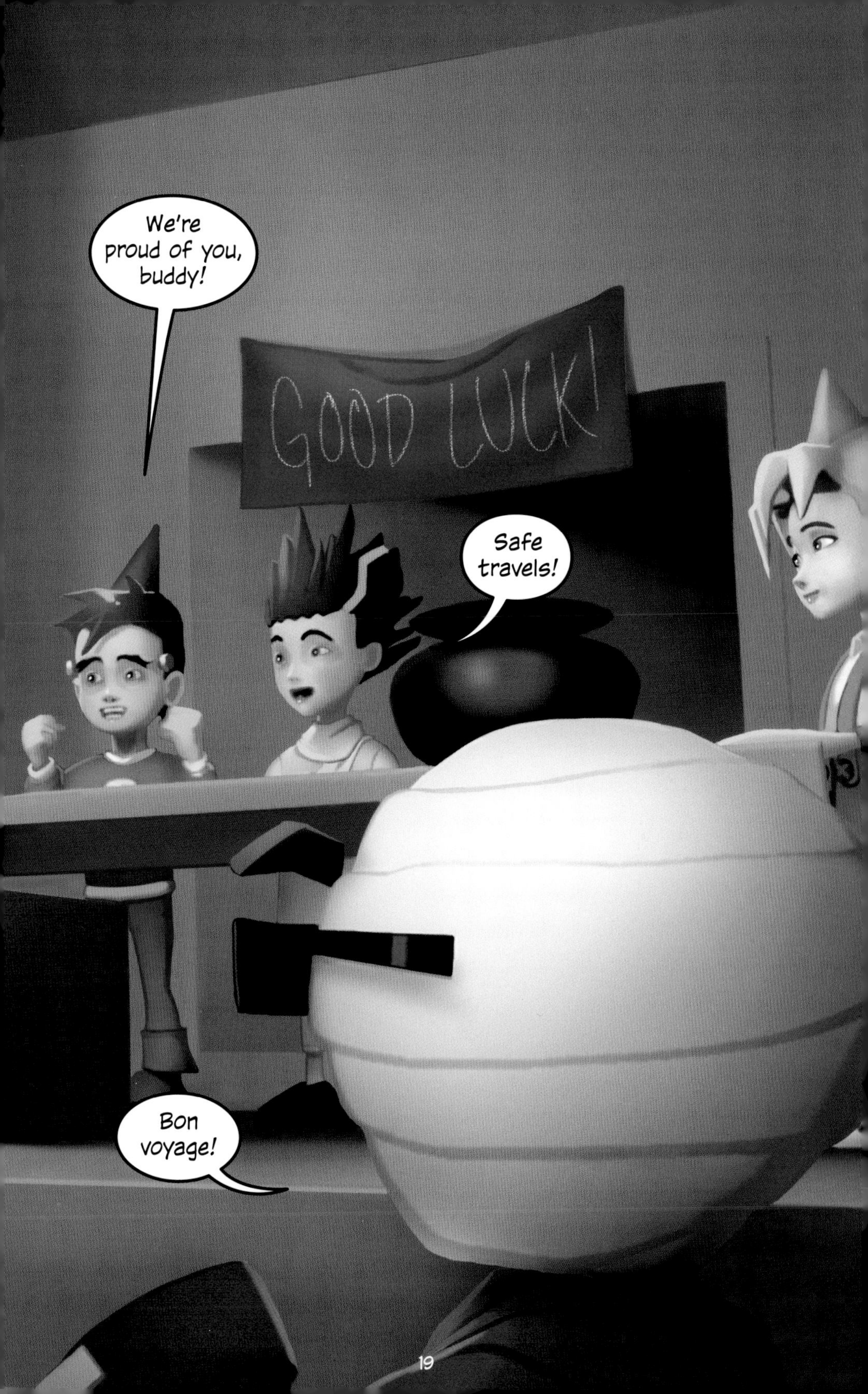
We're proud of you, buddy!
GOOD LUCK!
Safe travels!
Bon voyage!

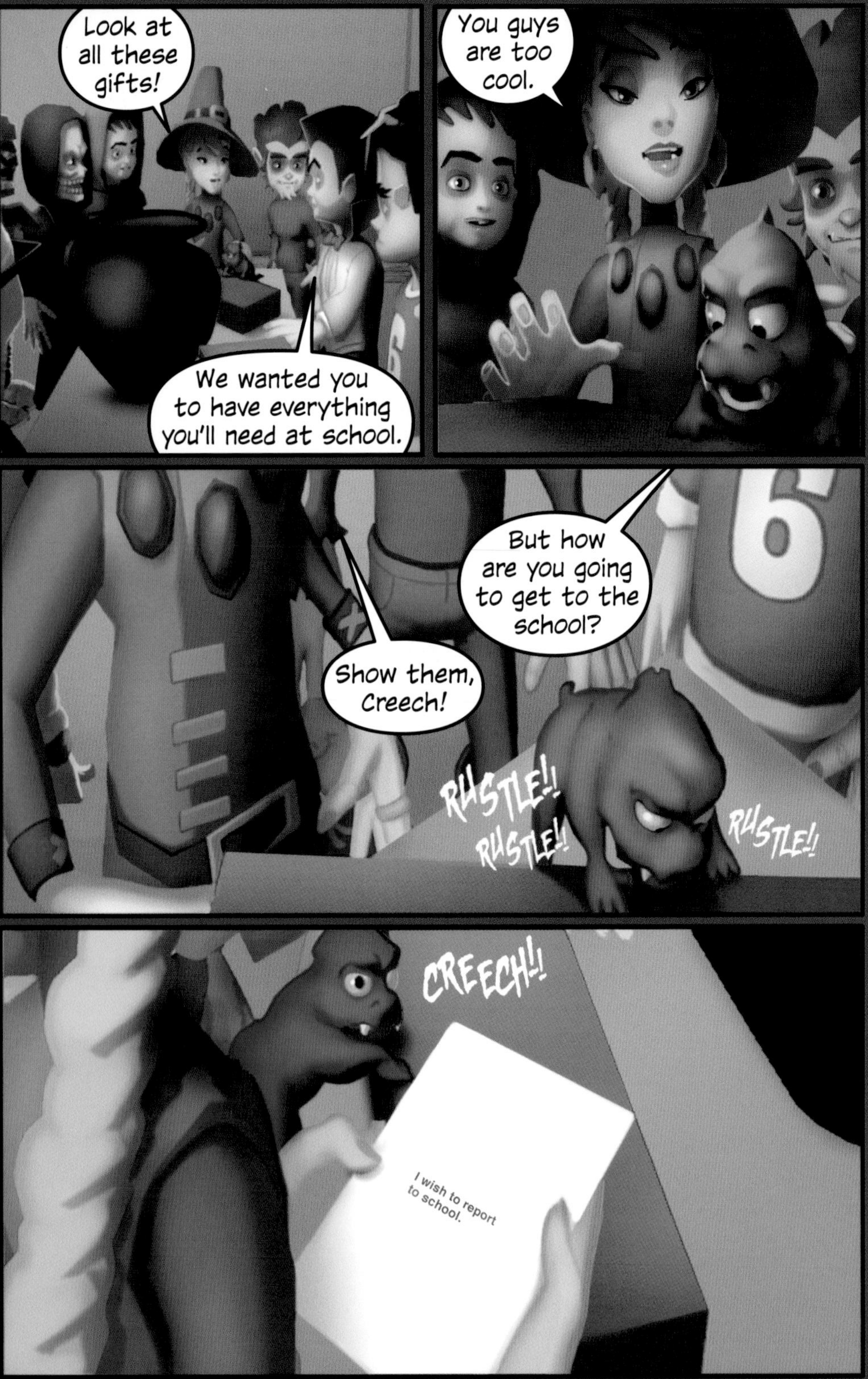
Look at all these gifts!
We wanted you to have everything you'll need at school.
You guys are too cool.
But how are you going to get to the school?
Show them, Creech!
RUSTLE!!
RUSTLE!!
RUSTLE!!
CREECH!!
I wish to report to school.

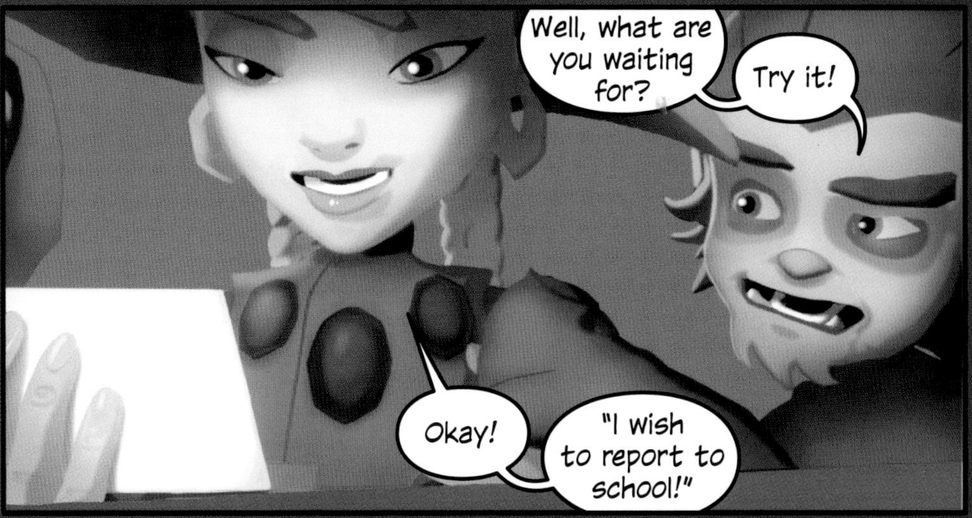
Well, what are you waiting for?
Try it!
Okay!
"I wish to report to school!"

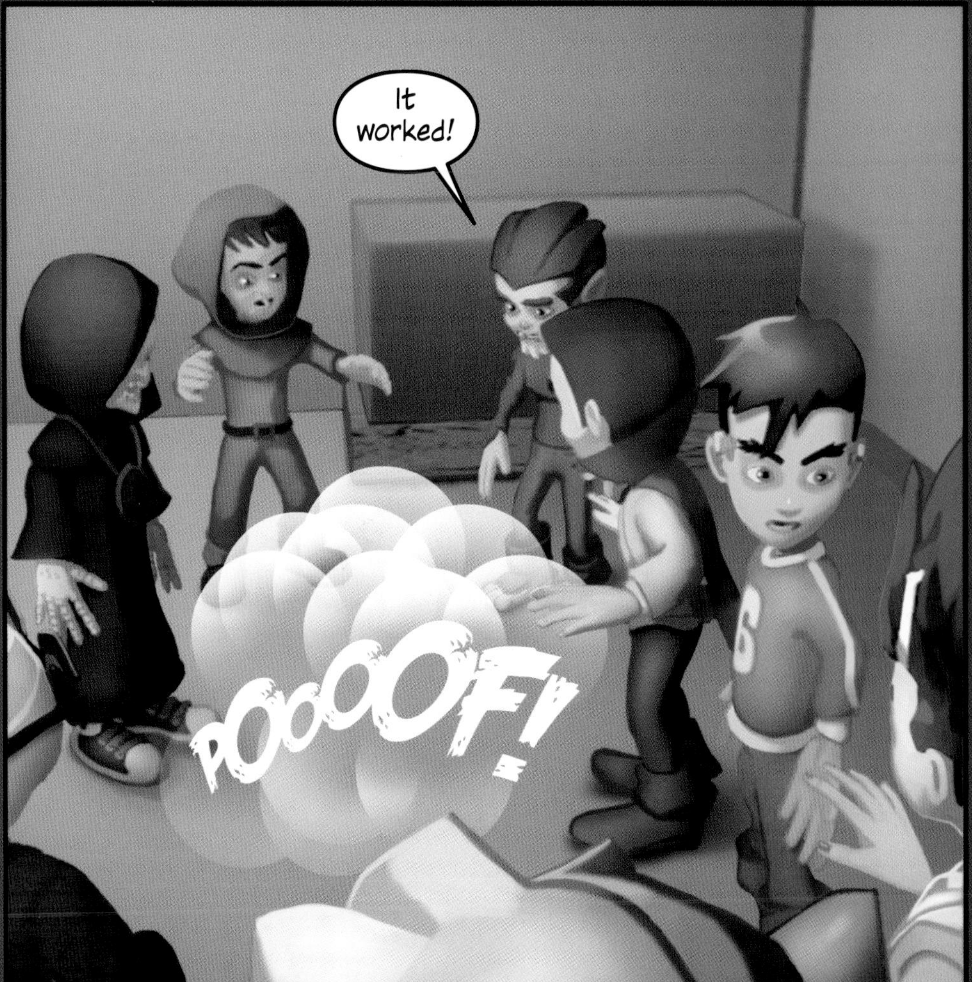
It worked!
POOOOF!

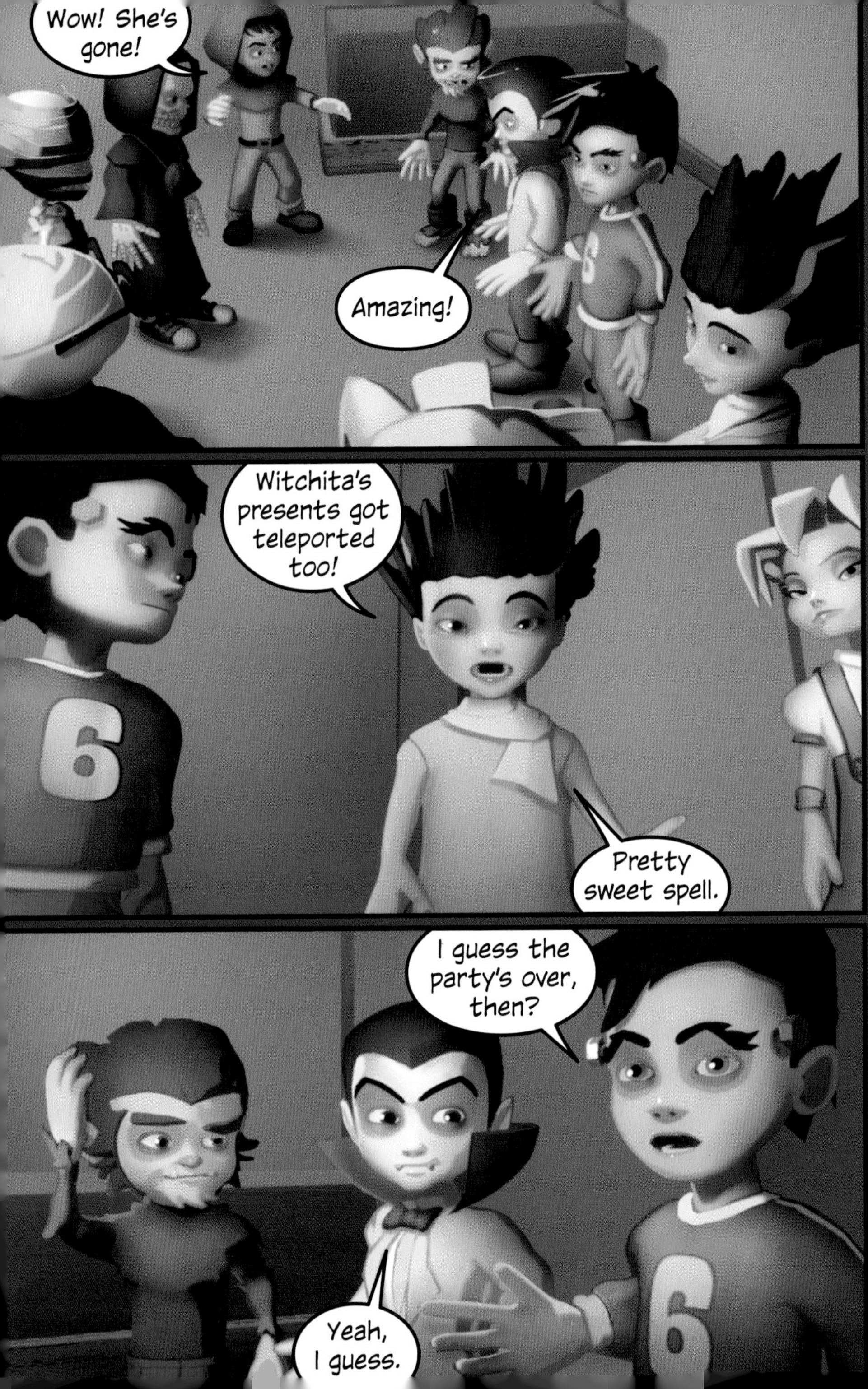
Wow! She's gone!
Amazing!
Witchita's presents got teleported too!
Pretty sweet spell.
I guess the party's over, then?
Yeah, I guess.

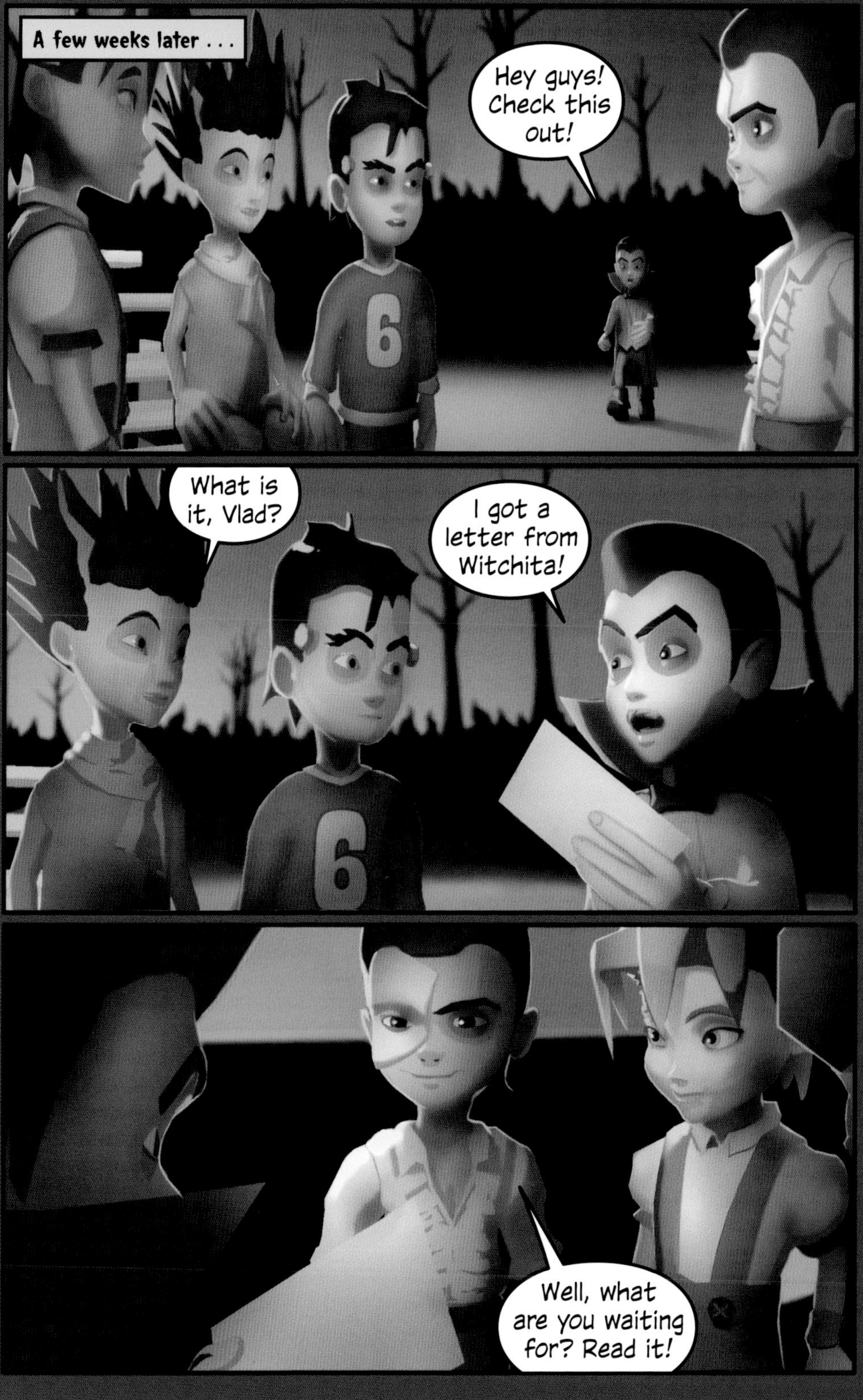
A few weeks later . . .
Hey guys! Check this out!
What is it, Vlad?
I got a letter from Witchita!
Well, what are you waiting for? Read it!

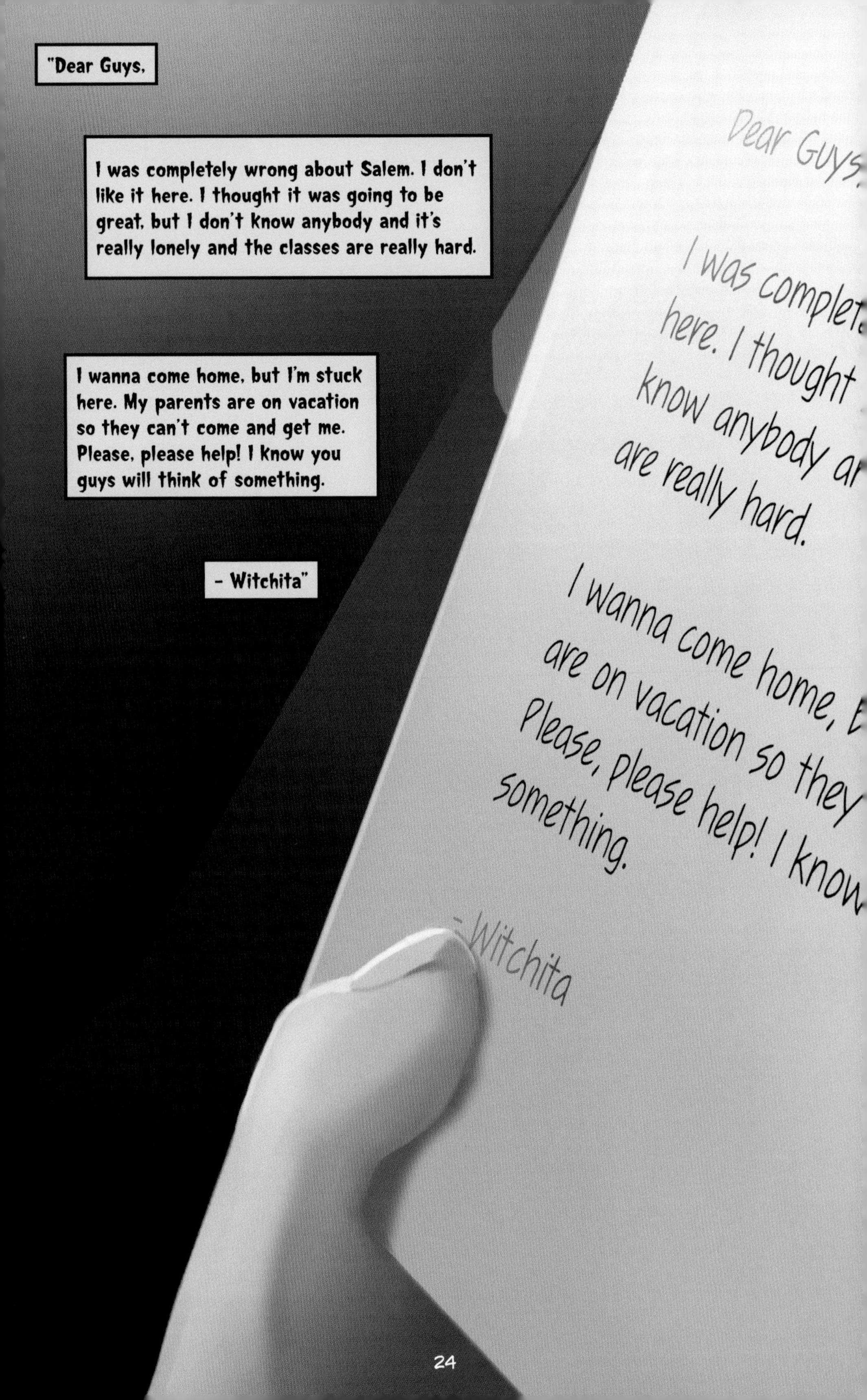
"Dear Guys,
I was completely wrong about Salem. I don't like it here. I thought it was going to be great, but I don't know anybody and it's really lonely and the classes are really hard.
I wanna come home, but I'm stuck here. My parents are on vacation so they can't come and get me. Please, please help! I know you guys will think of something.
- Witchita"

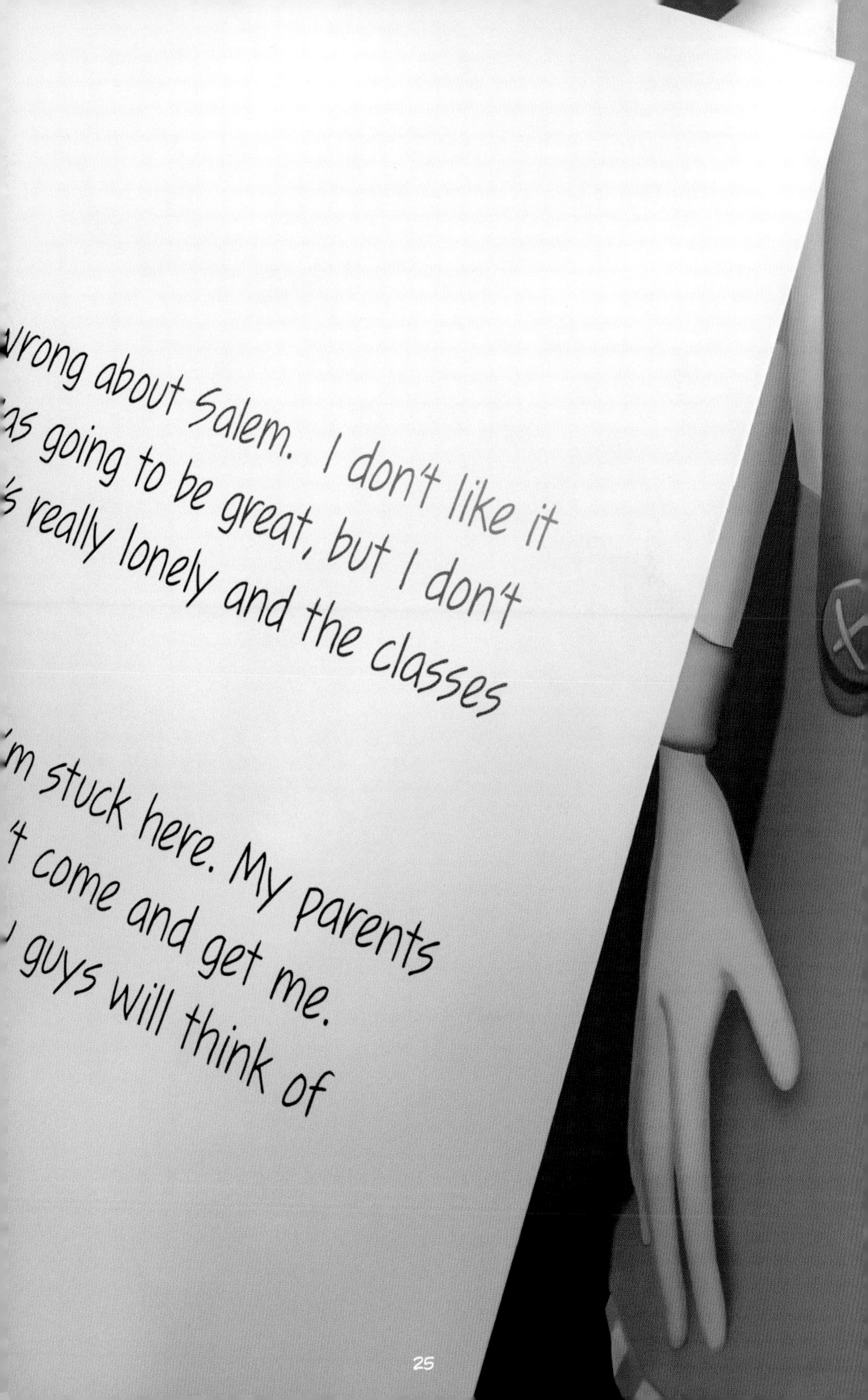
wrong about Salem. I don't like it
as going to be great, but I don't
s really lonely and the classes
m stuck here. My parents
t come and get me.
guys will think of

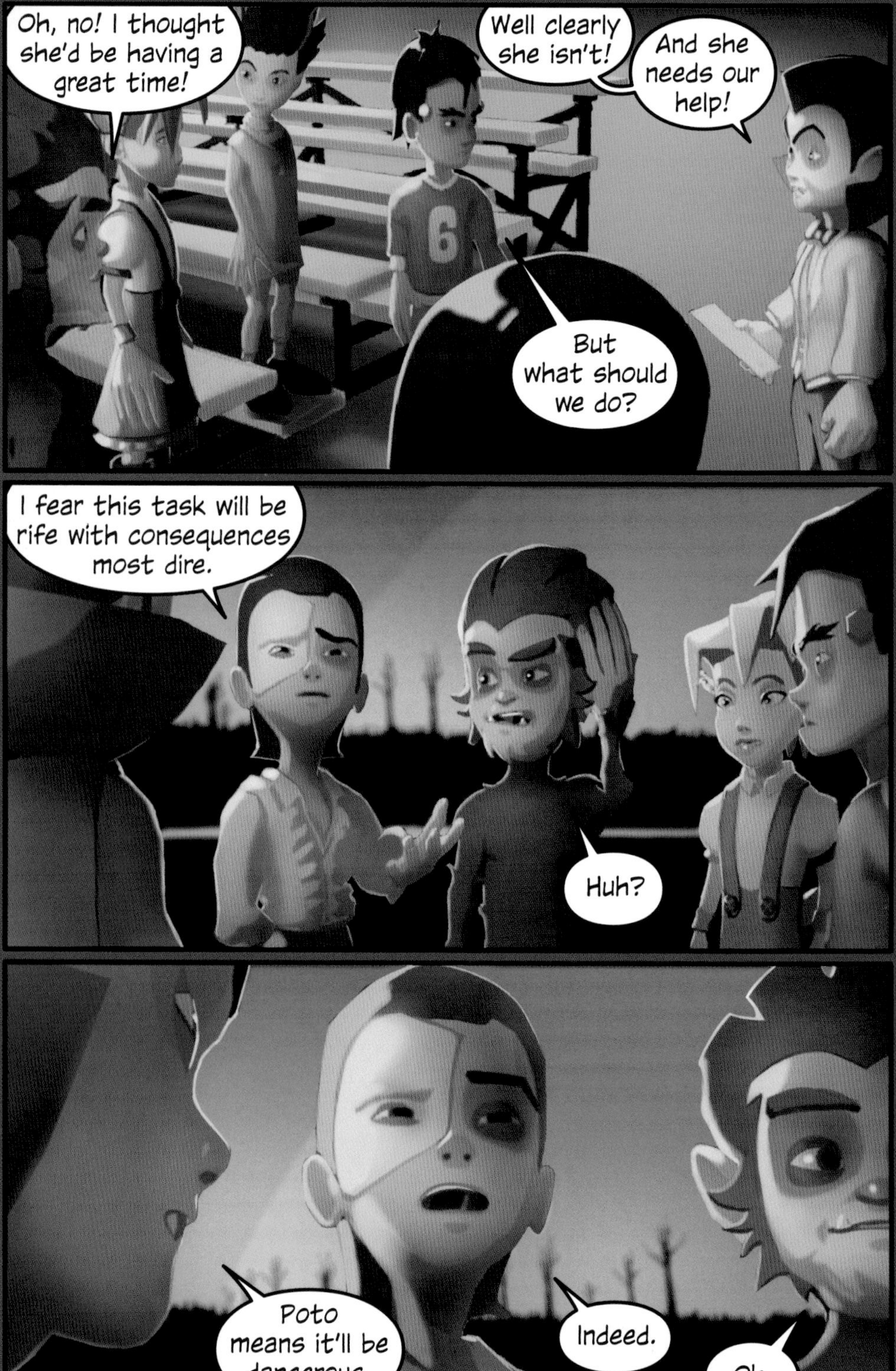
Oh, no! I thought she'd be having a great time!
Well clearly she isn't!
And she needs our help!
But what should we do?
I fear this task will be rife with consequences most dire.
Huh?
Poto means it'll be dangerous.
Indeed.
Oh.

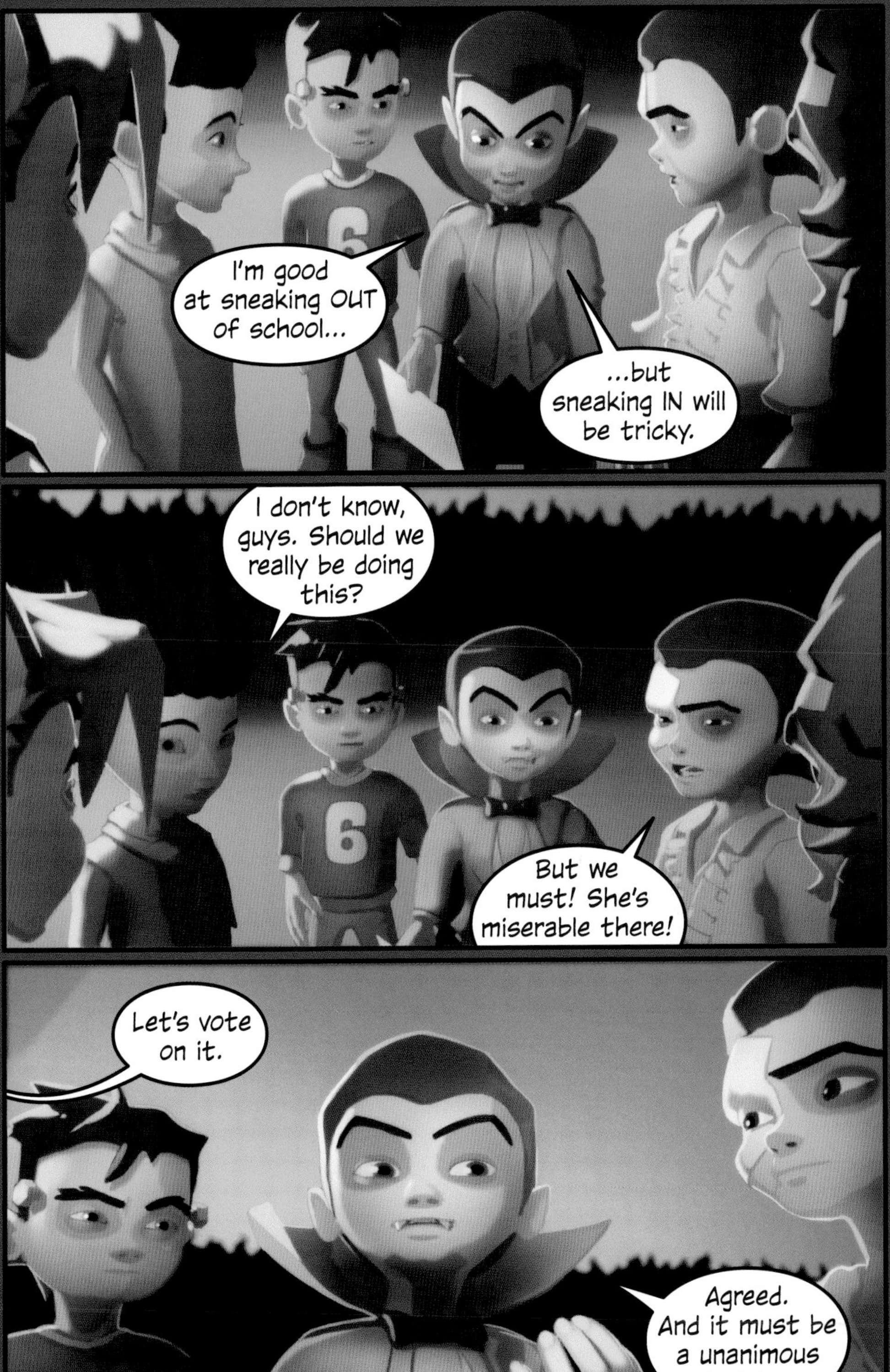
I'm good at sneaking OUT of school...
...but sneaking IN will be tricky.
I don't know, guys. Should we really be doing this?
But we must! She's miserable there!
Let's vote on it.
Agreed. And it must be a unanimous decision.

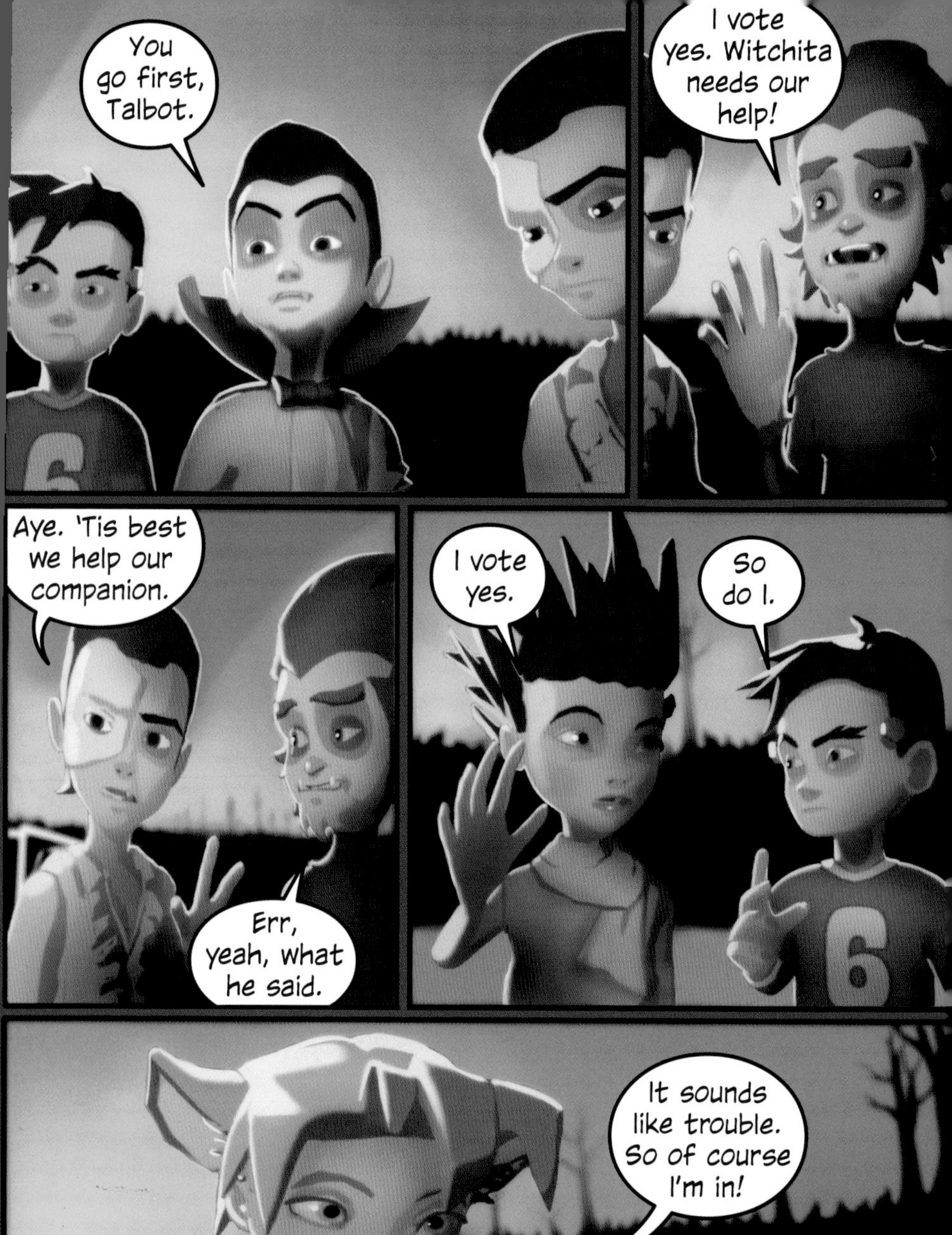
You go first, Talbot.
I vote yes. Witchita needs our help!
Aye. 'Tis best we help our companion.
Err, yeah, what he said.
I vote yes.
So do I.
It sounds like trouble. So of course I'm in!

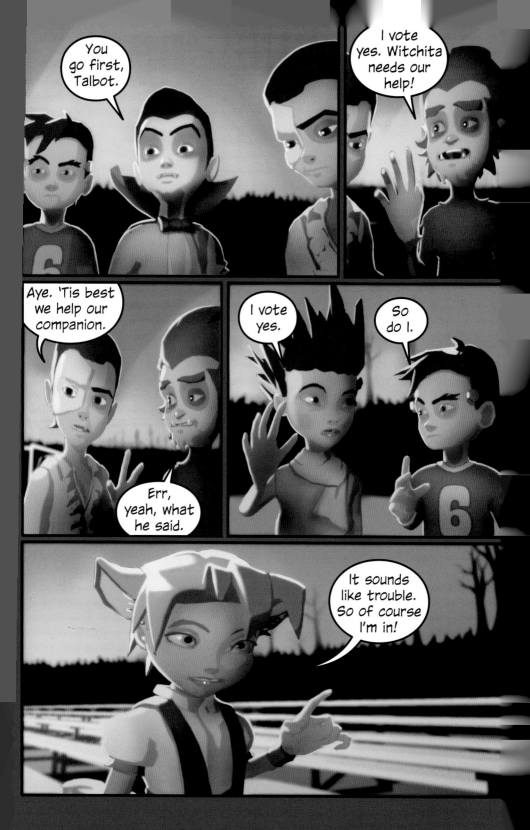

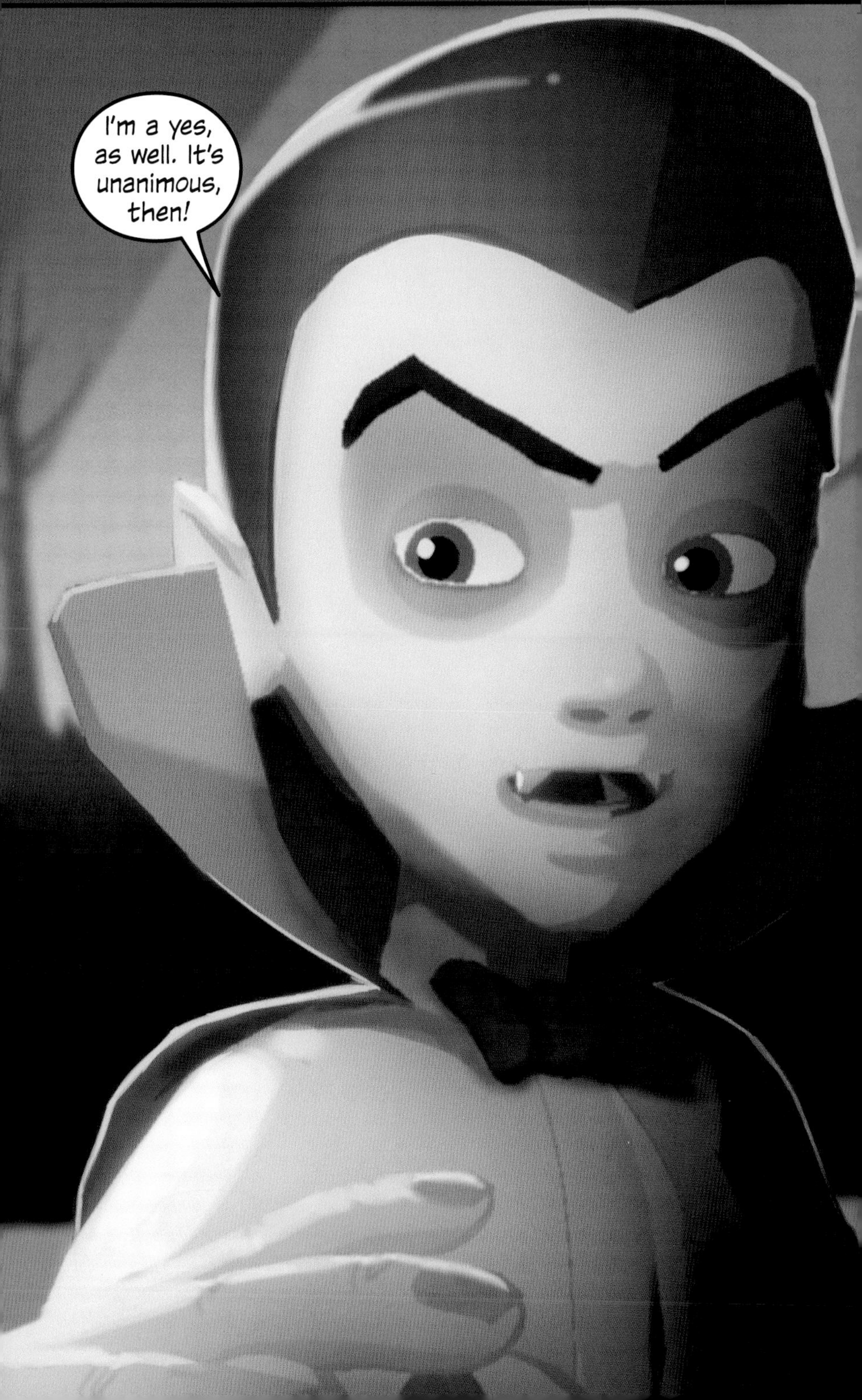
I'm a yes, as well. It's unanimous, then!

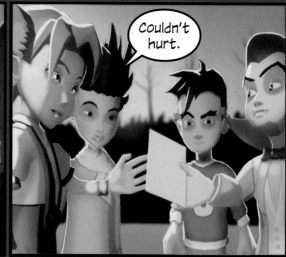

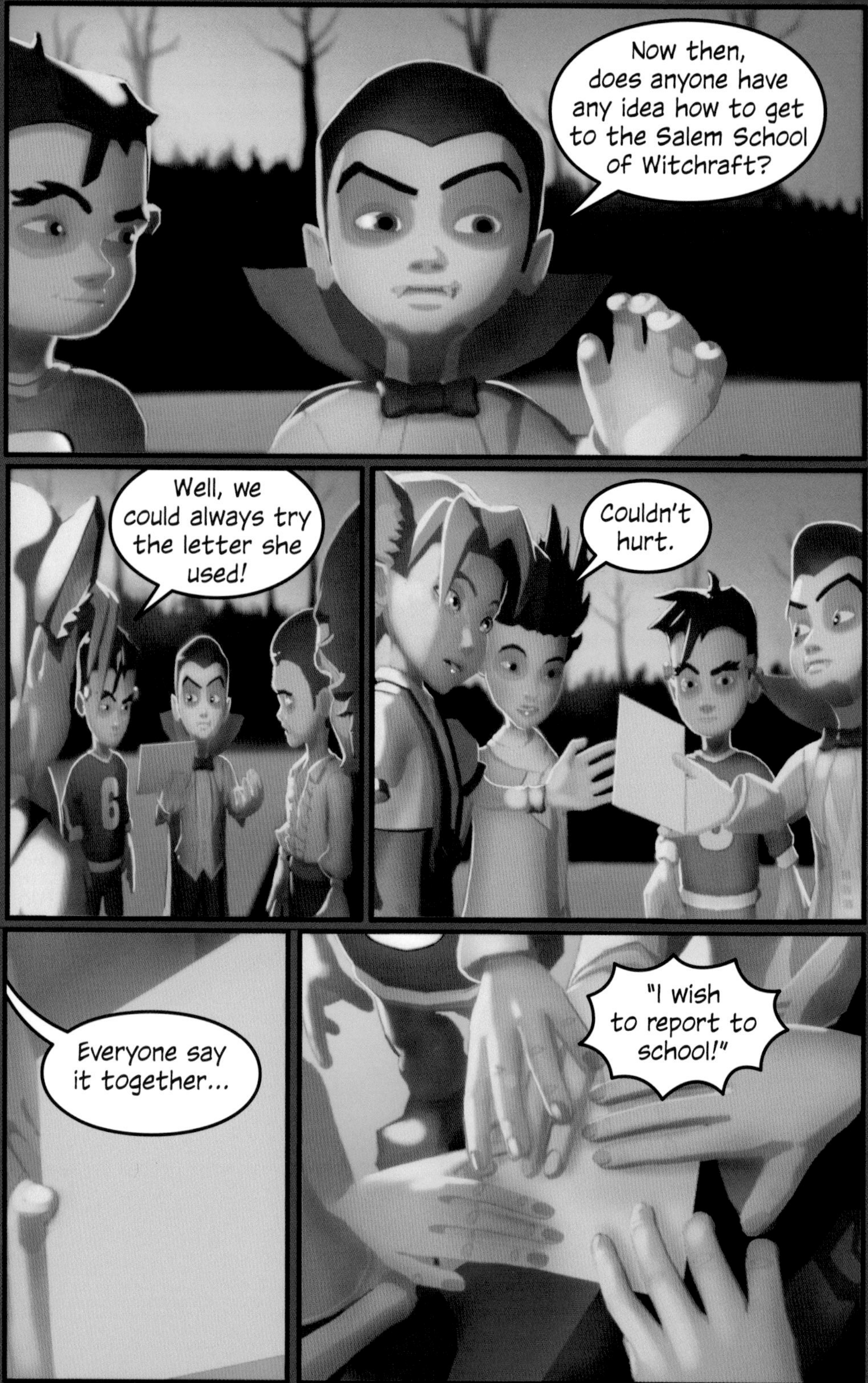

Now then, does anyone have any idea how to get to the Salem School of Witchraft?

Well, we could always try the letter she used!

Couldn't hurt.

Everyone say it together...

"I wish to report to school!"

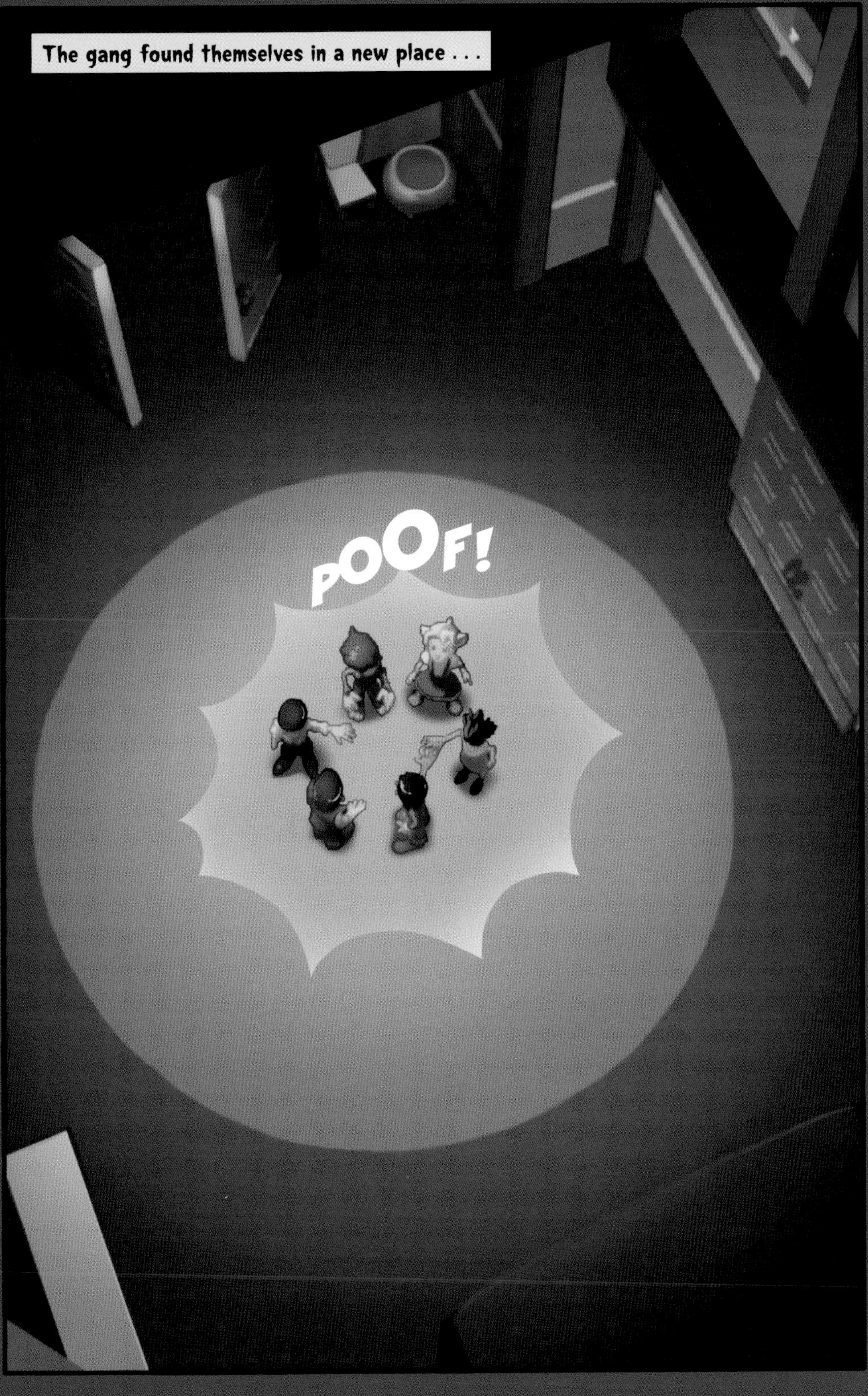
The gang found themselves in a new place . . .
POOF!

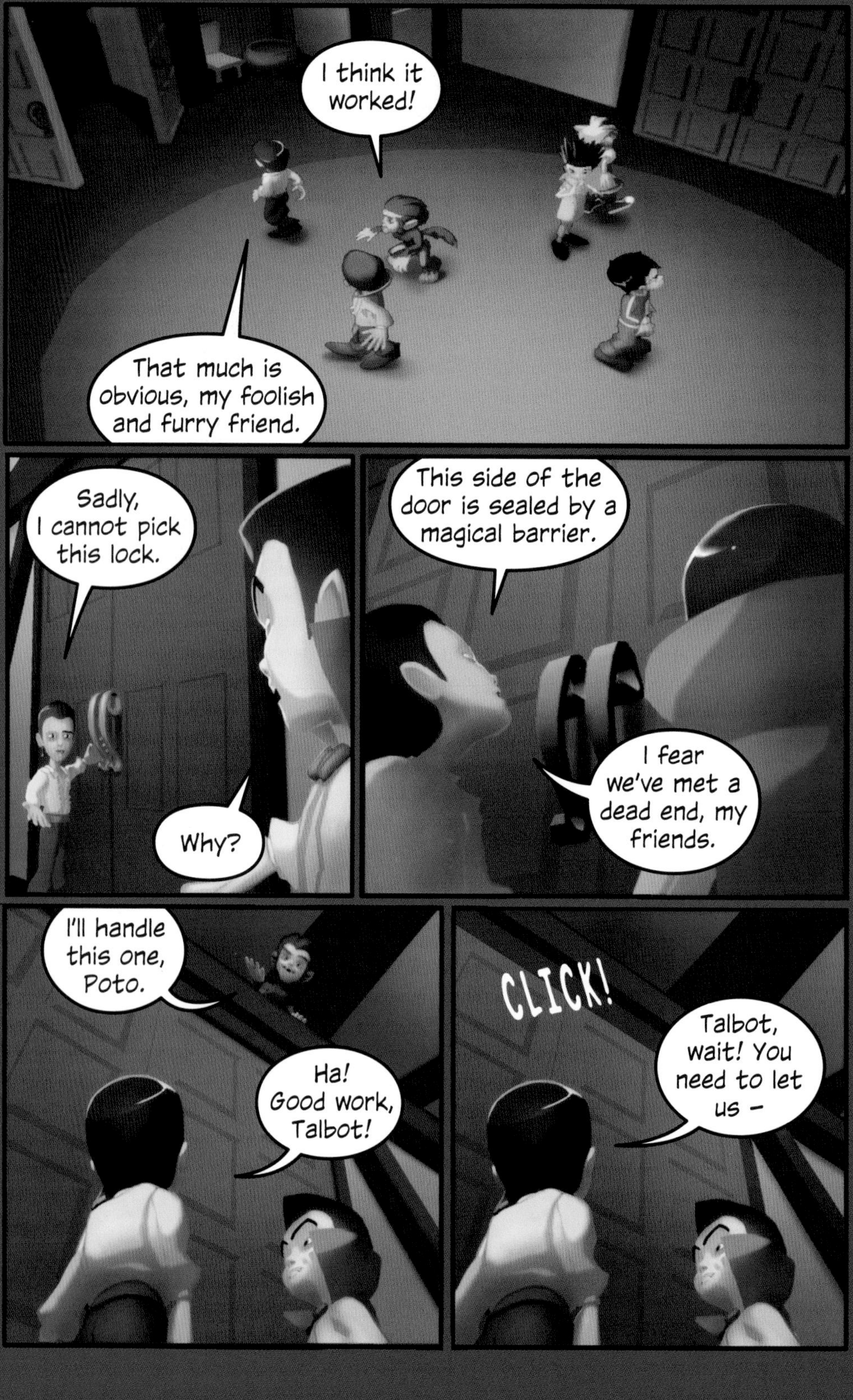
I think it worked!
That much is obvious, my foolish and furry friend.
Sadly, I cannot pick this lock.
Why?
This side of the door is sealed by a magical barrier.
I fear we've met a dead end, my friends.
I'll handle this one, Poto.
Ha! Good work, Talbot!
CLICK!
Talbot, wait! You need to let us –

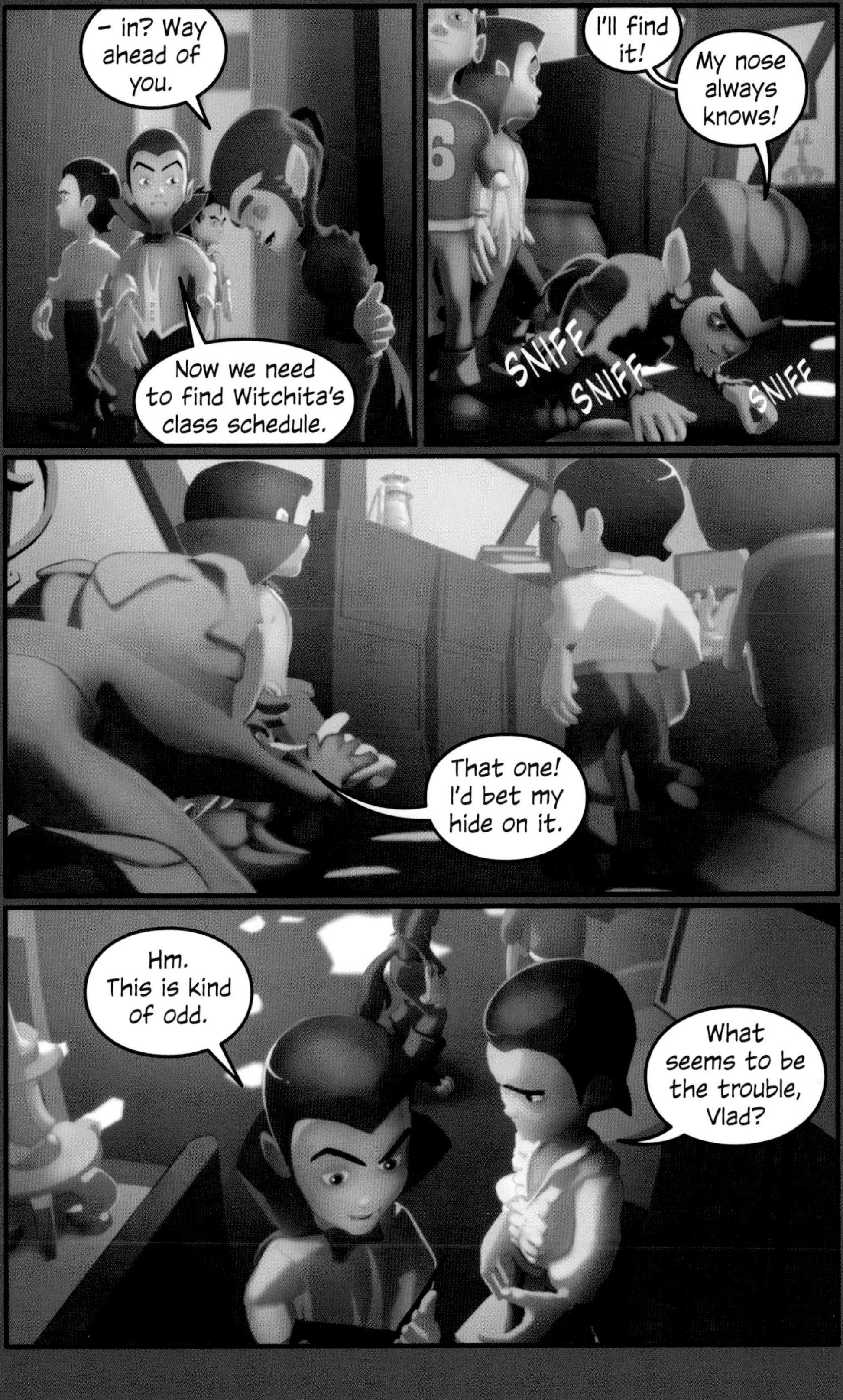
– in? Way ahead of you.
Now we need to find Witchita's class schedule.
I'll find it!
My nose always knows!
SNIFF
SNIFF
SNIFF
That one! I'd bet my hide on it.
Hm. This is kind of odd.
What seems to be the trouble, Vlad?

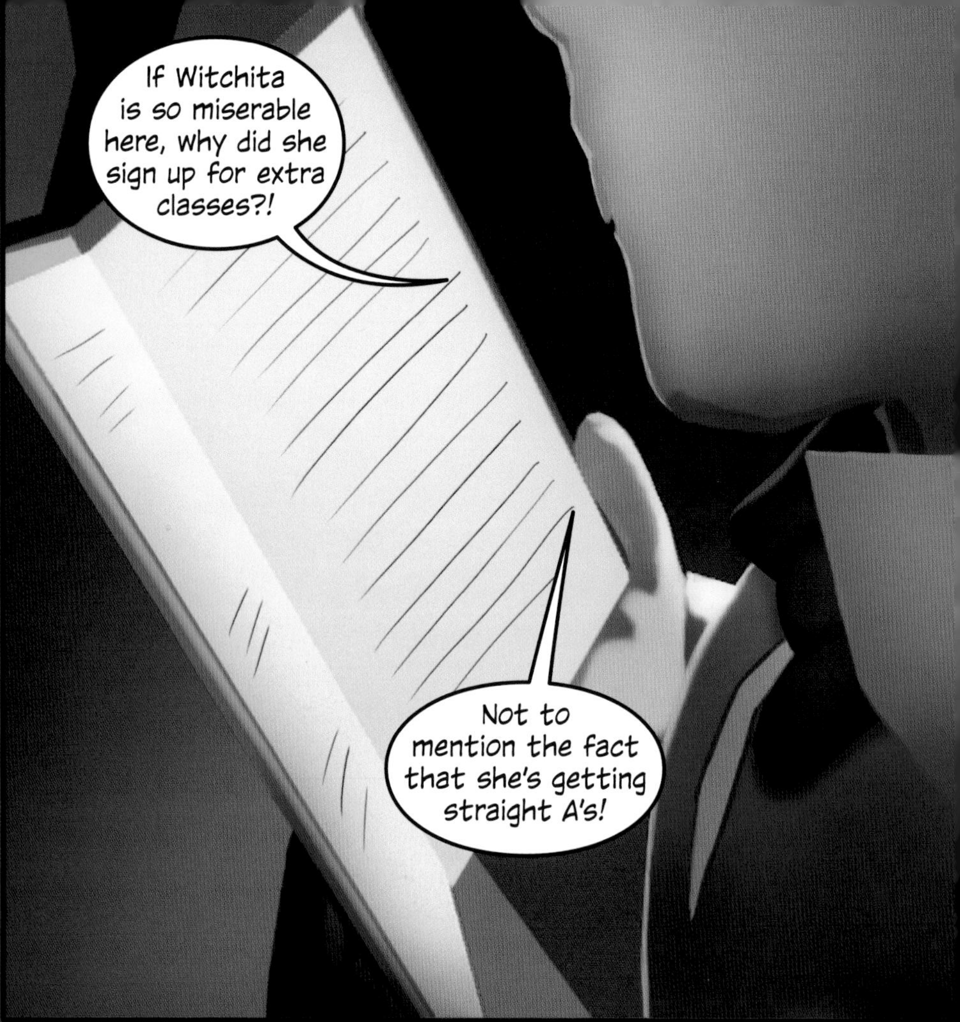
If Witchita is so miserable here, why did she sign up for extra classes?!
Not to mention the fact that she's getting straight A's!

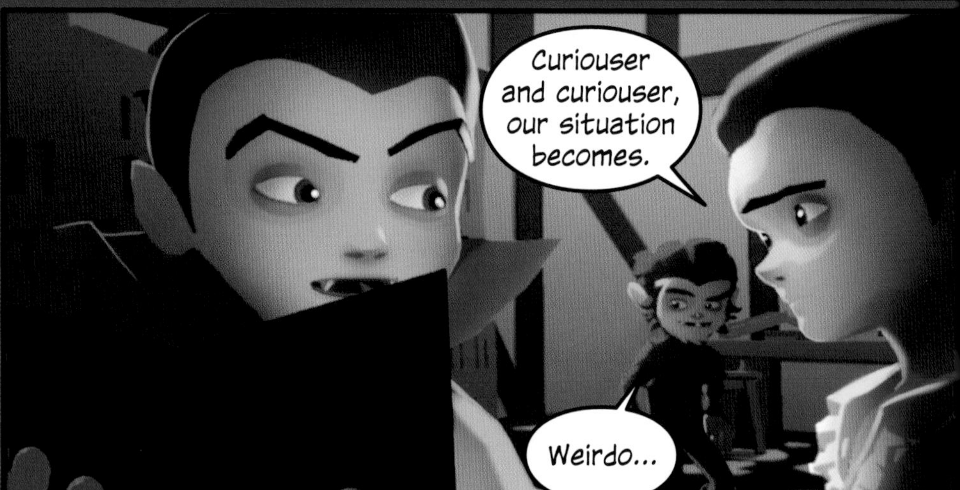
Curiouser and curiouser, our situation becomes.
Weirdo...

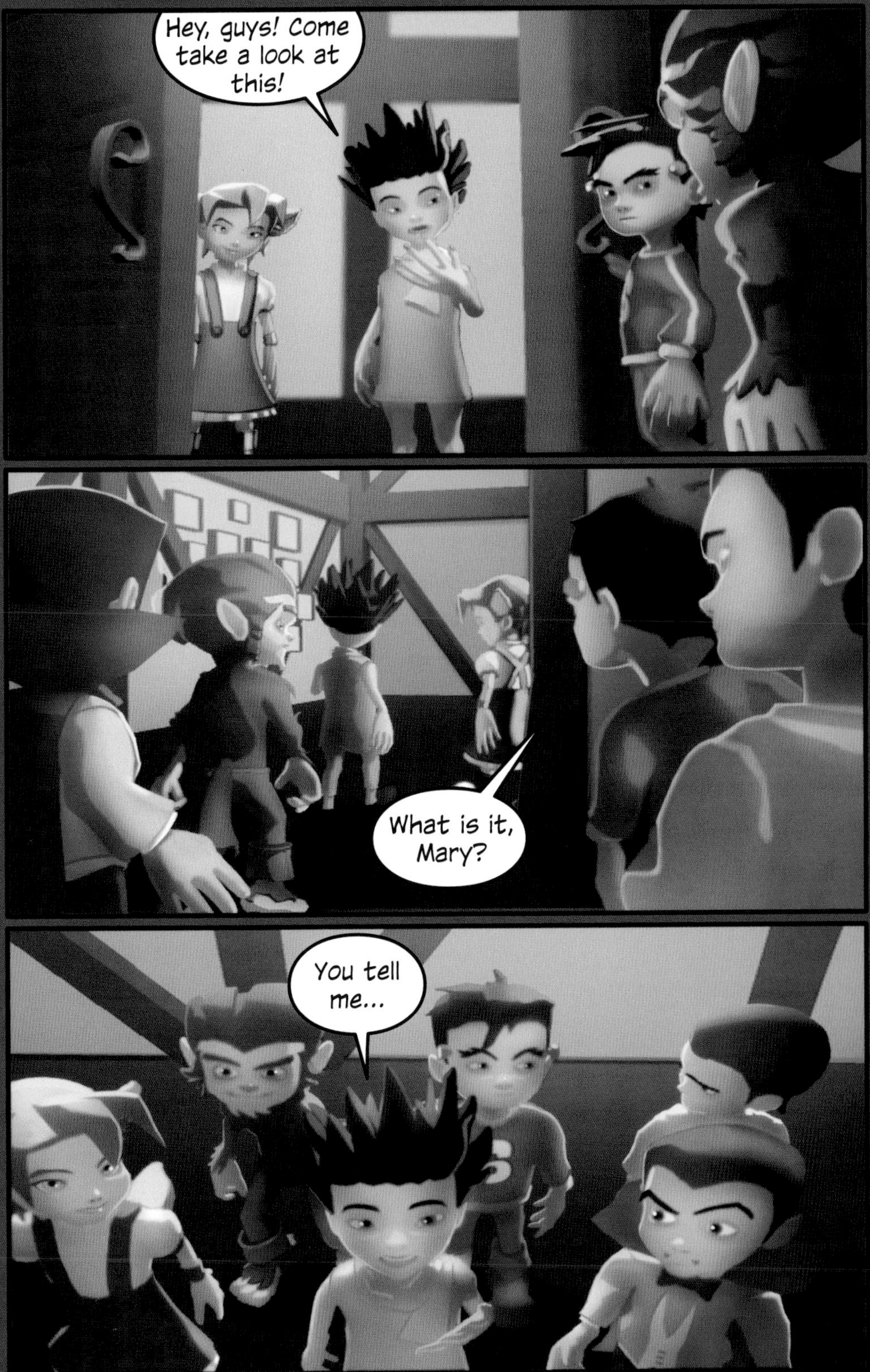
Hey, guys! Come take a look at this!
What is it, Mary?
You tell me...

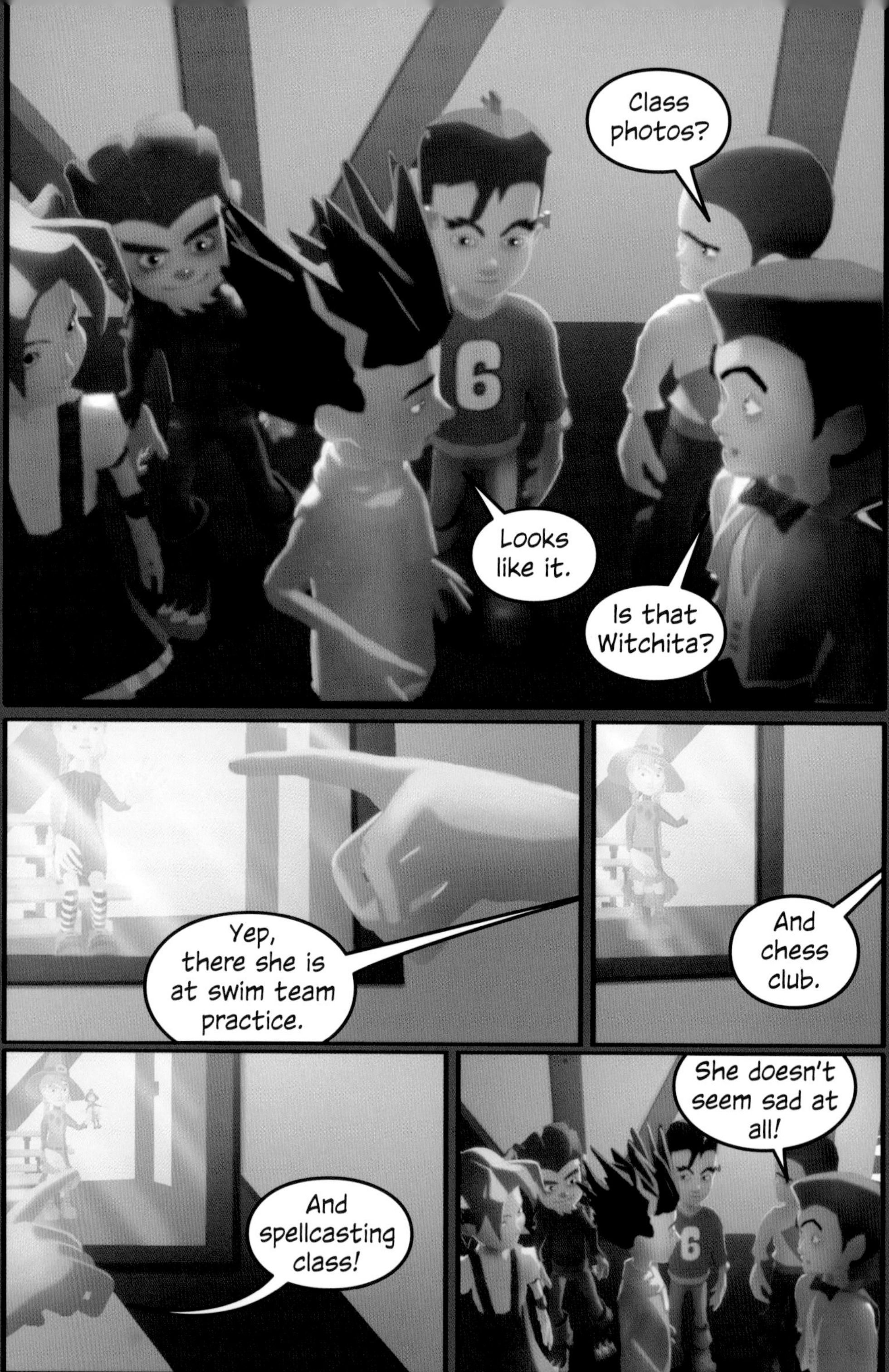
Class photos?
Looks like it.
Is that Witchita?
Yep, there she is at swim team practice.
And chess club.
And spellcasting class!
She doesn't seem sad at all!

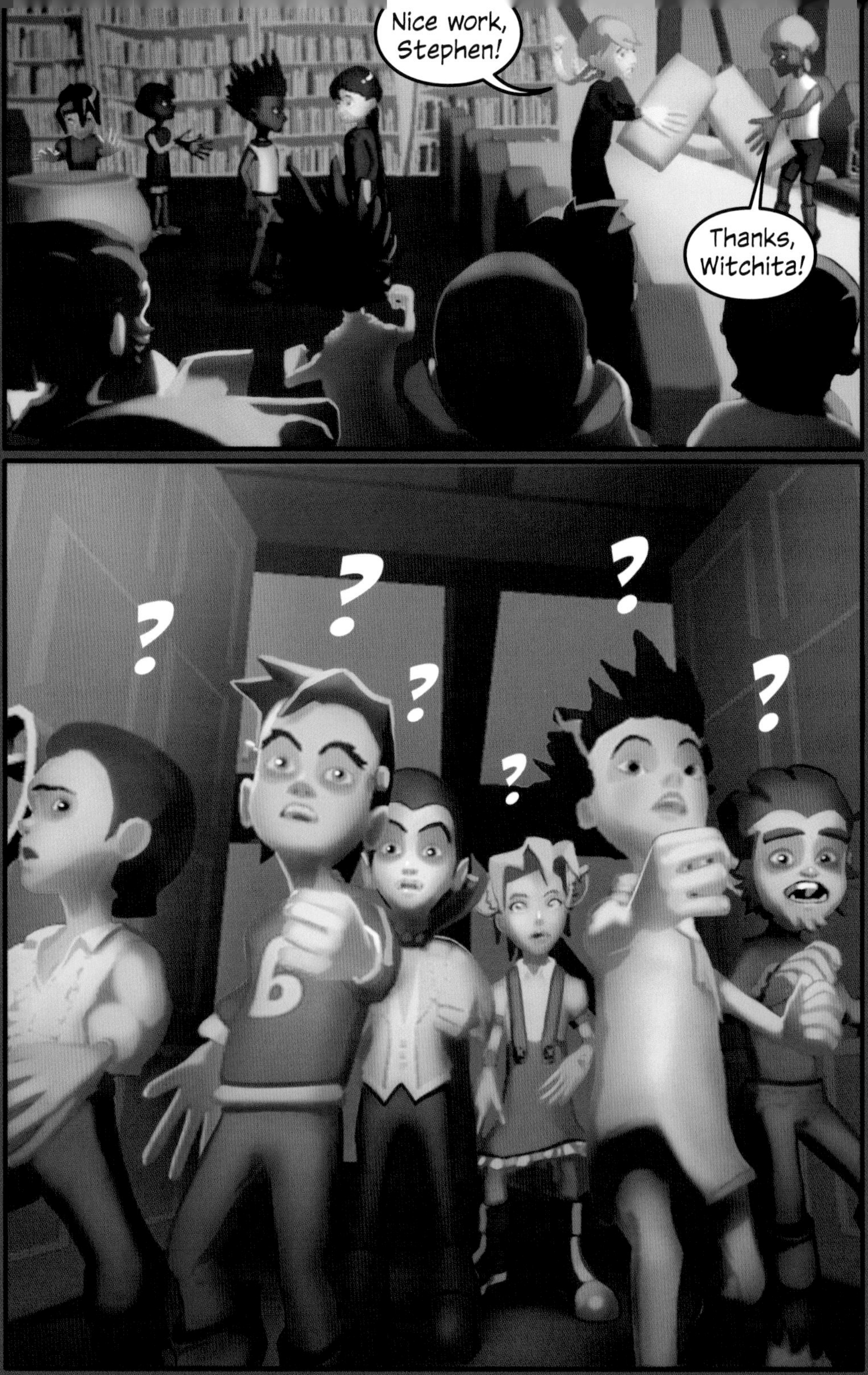
Nice work, Stephen!
Thanks, Witchita!
?
?
?
?
?
?

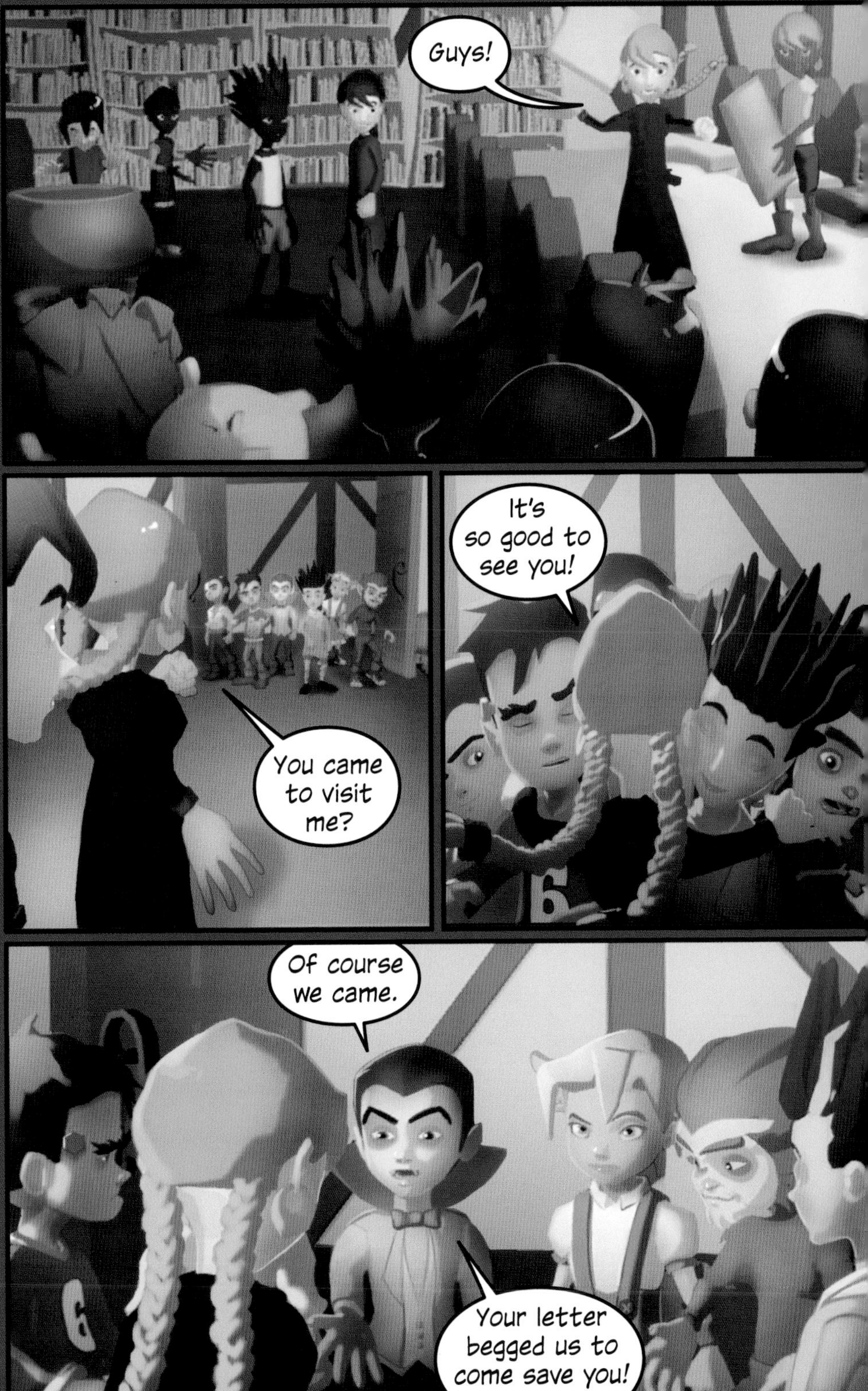
Guys!
You came to visit me?
It's so good to see you!
Of course we came.
Your letter begged us to come save you!

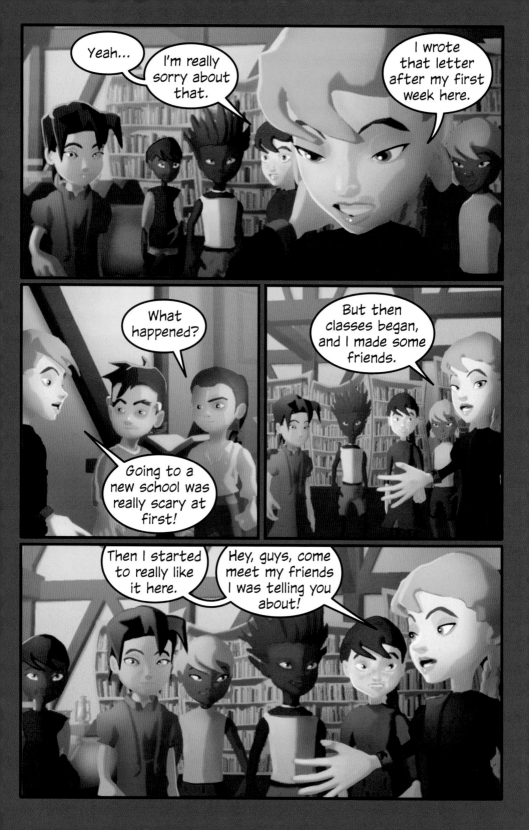

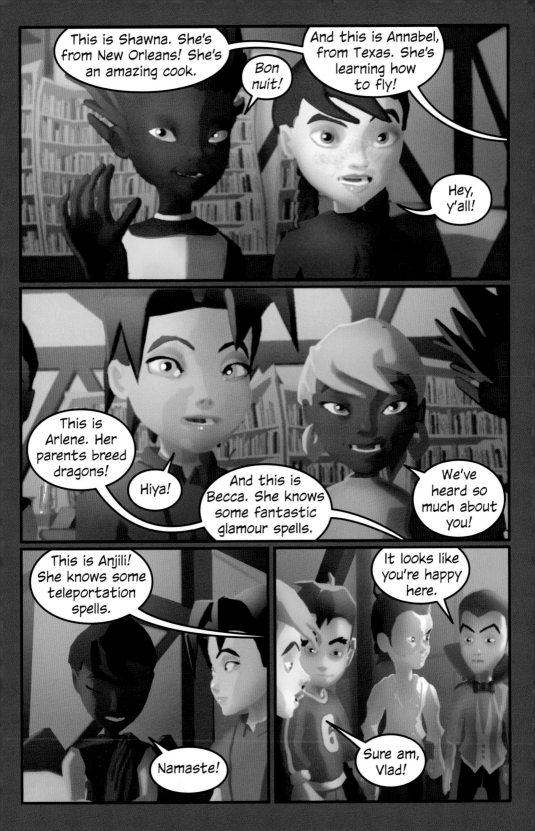

41

ABOUT
SEAN O'REILLY
AND ARCANA STUDIO

As a lifelong comics fan, Sean O'Reilly dreamed of becoming a comic book creator. In 2004, he realized that dream by creating Arcana Studio. In one short year, O'Reilly took his studio from a one-person operation in his basement to an award-winning comic book publisher with more than 150 graphic novels produced for Harper Collins, Simon & Schuster, Random House, Scholastic, and others.

Within a year, the company won many awards including the Shuster Award for Outstanding Publisher and the Moonbeam Award for top children's graphic novel. O'Reilly also won the Top 40 Under 40 award from the city of Vancouver and authored The Clockwork Girl for Top Graphic Novel at Book Expo America in 2009. Currently, O'Reilly is one of the most prolific independent comic book writers in Canada. While showing no signs of slowing down in comics, he now writes screenplays and adapts his creations for the big screen.

GLOSSARY

accepted (ak-SEP-tid)—if you are accepted into something, you have been allowed to join

barrier (BA-ree-ur)—a bar, fence, or wall that prevents people, traffic, or other things from going past it

consequences (KON-suh-kwen-siz)—the results of an action

dire (DYE-ur)—dreadful or urgent

gifted (GIFT-id)—if you are gifted at doing something, you have a natural ability to do it

miserable (MIZ-ur-uh-buhl)—sad, unhappy, or dejected

obvious (OB-vee-uhss)—easy to see or understand

rife (RIFE)—abundant, plentiful, or filled with something

teleported (TEL-uh-port-id)—moved from one location to another instantly

unanimous (yoo-NAN-uh-muhss)—agreed on by everyone

DISCUSSION QUESTIONS

1. Which one of the Mighty Mighty Monsters is your favorite? Why?

2. Witchita teleports to school. Where would you go if you could teleport anywhere? Talk about traveling.

3. The gang votes to go save Witchita from summer school. Is voting a good or bad way to solve problems? Discuss your answers.

WRITING PROMPTS

1. Imagine that you have to go to summer school. What kind of school would you go to? What would you want to learn? Write about your summer at school.

2. Each Mighty Mighty Monster has his or her own set of special skills. Imagine yourself as a monster. What kind of monster are you? What skills do you have? Write about it, then draw a picture of your monstrous self.

3. Witchita has lots of friends. How many friends do you have? Do you wish you had more? Less? What is the best amount of friends to have? Why? Write about friends.

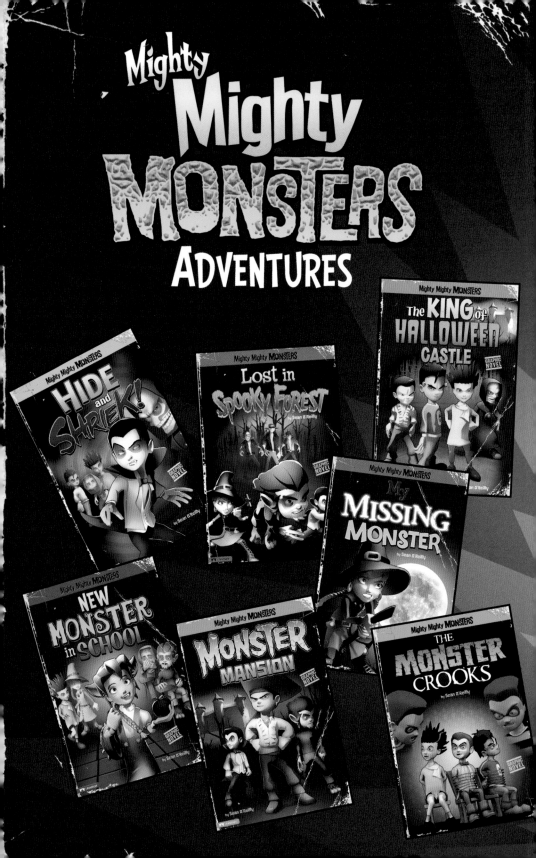